Beautiful disaster

Tommy B. Lay

Copyright © 2023 by Tommy B. Lay

All rights reserved.

No portion of this book may be reproduced in any form without written permission from the publisher or author, except as permitted by U.S. copyright law.

Contents

Prologue	1
1. Chapter 1	11
2. Chapter 2	20
3. Chapter 3	35
4. Chapter 4	43
5. Chapter 5	50
6. Chapter 6	55
7. Chapter 7	66
8. Chapter 8	74
9. Chapter 9	81
10. Chapter 10	86
11. Chapter 11	93
12. Chapter 12	99

13. Chapter 13 — 102
14. Chapter 14 — 108
15. Chapter 15 — 113
16. Chapter 16 — 118
17. Chapter 17 — 122
18. Chapter 18 — 129
19. Chapter 19 — 135
20. Chapter 20 — 141
21. Chapter 21 — 149
22. Chapter 22 — 162
23. Chapter 23 — 172
24. Chapter 24 — 179
25. Chapter 25 — 198
26. Chapter 26 — 217
27. Chapter 27 — 226
28. Chapter 28 — 234
29. Chapter 29 — 244
30. Chapter 30 — 252
31. Epilogue — 261
32. Bonus Chapter — 273

Prologue

I had always been a good girl.

I followed what daddy said, submitted my homework on time, helped with the house chores, and took turns making breakfast.

Like I said, I had always been a good girl. However, my life changed when I met Adam.

I'm not even a part of the high school social hierarchy, but I'm not an outcast either. You've heard of the jocks, the nerds, and the wannabes. Well as for me, I just belong in the 'everyone else' category aka average but cool.

So I had no idea why Adam, our famous high school's football quarterback, asked me to be his girlfriend. Me being 18 and oblivious, would of course say yes to him. Adam was my first boyfriend, not my first kiss, but the first guy I slept with.

I never told my dad about our relationship, and maybe I should have. Because now, looking at the pregnancy test in front of me, it reminds me that I'm no longer my daddy's good girl. Like, my actual dad, not sugar daddy you pervs. Though sometimes I think I do have a daddy kink, but that's a story for another time.

Anyway...

Positive

How am I supposed to tell Adam about this?

Suddenly I heard my bedroom door being open. My dad's head peek inside as he said, "Sweetheart, I ordered pizza for dinner. Come down so we could eat together."

My eyes were teary and I didn't want my dad to see so I quickly blink back a tear and discreetly pushed the pregnancy test under the pillow.

Oh god please don't let him see.

I'm a good girl. I'm a good girl. I'm a good girl.

"Sure dad, I'll be down in a minute."

"You okay?" asked my dad. "You look a bit pale, and-- were you crying?"

It's been 5 years since mom's death. It was hard for me to accept her death but my dad has been very supportive throughout these years. After all he's the only family that I have.

"I'm okay dad, and no, I'm not."

"Are you sure? You can't lie to this old man, sweetheart."

I smiled a little, "You're not that old, dad."

"Would you tell me what's wrong?" he asked while leaning forward to study me closely. "You don't look too good."

I tried to stay calm under his gaze.

"You're my only daughter and I vowed to your mom and myself that I will protect you." That's what he always said to me.

When I remember his words, I can't help but cry. Telling him about my pregnancy will cause a great pain. It will make me feel flawed and unlovable, when all I ever wanted was to feel loved and accepted.

"Dad, I-I'm..." It's hard for me to tell him that I'm pregnant. I don't want to break his heart.

My dad took my hand and squeezed it, "Hey sweetheart, it's okay you can tell me anything. Just let it out. Did anybody hurt you?"

I decided not to tell him. He would be so sad knowing that his only daughter is pregnant at such a young age.

Besides, we are not financially stable at the moment so I don't want to add his burden and let him stressing out on how to help me to raise this child.

"It's nothing actually. School is just stressing me out, that's all. Besides, it's my senior year so you know..." I told him, hoping he didn't see through me and know that I was lying.

The tension on my dad's face finally faded a little, "Ahh, yes. Don't worry sweetheart, there's only a few months left. It will all be over after you graduate soon, okay?"

I let out a chuckle, "Yeah, thanks dad. I think I'm okay now. So, let's eat that pizza now?" I asked him with a smile, trying to sound happy again.

Who knows, this might be our last dinner together.

The next morning I woke up early to meet Adam. I look at the time on my wristwatch and thankful that it was 8:30 which means Adam's parents probably have went to work. We are also lucky that we didn't have a class today.

Once I have arrived at his house, I rang the doorbell and waited. After Adam opened the door and let me inside, I went straight to his bedroom while pulling him with me.

"Woah babe, it's still early in the morning but you already miss me? Looks like someone is eager to have me again." Adam said, he was obviously smirking as he said that and I don't have to look back to know it. I only rolled my eyes at his words.

I closed the door to his bedroom and pulled him to sit beside me on his bed.

I looked at Adam intently and thinking on how should I break the news to him but then decided to just go with it. "Listen, I have something very, very important to tell you."

Adam only let out a small laugh. He obviously didn't take it seriously.

Ugh this guy.

"Alright fine, so what is it? What's so important babe?" he asked.

"Adam, I just found out about this last night. I didn't tell anyone, not even my dad. Oh god, especially not him. Only god knows what would happened if he knew." I said in a rush, trying not to show how scared I am, but seeing the reaction on Adam's face tell me that I obviously failed.

After he figured out my panic state, Adam decided to look serious and waiting for what I am about to say next.

"Adam, I'm actually... it's uh,"

"Come on, Jane. Don't scare me, just say it!" Adam insisted.

I look into his eyes and I guess he can already tell what I am about to say to him.

"I'm pregnant." There, I finally told him. Great, so now we both can start planning on what to do next.

Honestly, I had expected for Adam to scream at me and throw off things or something but I clearly didn't expect this.

He looked at me with a smirk until it turns into a smile and then into a laugh.

So... Adam was laughing right now. Does that means he is okay that I am pregnant? So he wants this child as well right?

"So, you're okay with this?" I asked him.

But Adam seemed to still be indulge in laughter. Not knowing what to say, I kept quiet, but slid close.

Adam looked at me, "What? You pregnant? With my child? Ha! Good one, Jane. That's definitely a joke right?"

He thinks this is a joke?

"Adam, I'm serious! This is not a joke. I'm actually pregnant! God!" I told him.

Adam's face turns pale and he looked scared.

He pace back and forth in his room while I was still sitting on his bed and looking at him curiously.

He deliberately push things off of the table and nudge them from the shelves onto the floor.

I looked at him with wide eyes. So my expectation of him was right all along.

I sighed and frowned at his behavior right now. "Stop it, Adam! What is wrong with you?" I screamed.

Adam abruptly stop what he was doing and turn to look at me.

"What is wrong with me? You asked me what is wrong with me? Damn it, Jane! What is wrong with you? You just told me y-you were pregnant and you asked me what's wrong? This is all wrong! I-I don't want to have a child. I'm too young to be a dad." Adam screamed at me, his face was contorted in rage and anger.

I was stunned at his words, "Now what? I'm pregnant, Adam! And god help me because my dad would totally kill me if he finds out about this, not just the fact that I'm dating someone but I'm also pregnant!"

"Shit I don't know, Jane. Just abort it or whatever! I'm not raising that child." He said, sounding disgusted.

To say that I was shocked would be an understatement, "You want me to abort this baby? Our baby? What the hell, Adam? No! I'm not doing that, I don't want to kill this baby!"

"Well if you have a better idea then please tell me because I'm pretty sure abortion is the only way for us to solve this problem!"

"Adam, we are both still young but if you're willing to go through this with me, together we could raise this child and I'm sure we could work something out later. I could work at a cafe or wherever and we could save some money for our family and-"

"Woah okay, stop there, just stop. What? Our family? You're going too far now Jane. There's no our family or shit cause I'm not going there." Seeing the stunned look on my face, Adam grab me by the shoulders and look right into my eyes. "Look, here's my idea, you abort the baby or we're done. See? Simple right?" Adam told me.

Abort the baby or we're done?

"What? What do you mean we're done? I-I'm..." I stammered, trying not to think about the fact that my boyfriend just initiated that we should break up.

In this point, I can already see where this is going. I can see my future crumble right in front of me. I'm at my lowest point right now. In this second, I have come to the point that I think my life has turned into a complete disaster.

How can someone like me make such a hurtful mistake. I would totally blame this on being young and dumb.

Adam shake my shoulders to get my attention again, "Jane, it's either you get rid of the baby or you know, I can go my way while you go your way and I don't know just keep the baby since you want it so much."

"You want to break up?" I asked him. I feel like I already know the answer, but somehow I still hope there's a chance for Adam and me to still be together in the future and raise our baby together.

There are many young parents out there. I'm sure we could figure out a way too.

"Well I didn't say it but-"

I cut Adam off, "But that's exactly what you mean, right? I should have known. Of course you don't want this baby. You took my virginity Adam. You were my first. How could you do this?" I sighed, shaking my head in disbelief.

Adam grunts, "Damn it Jane! Stop making this hard. It's just your virginity, you're gonna lose it anyway. If you want that damn baby so much then go! I don't need you or that baby in my life!"

This is going just like how I imagined, but maybe if I try one more time he would change his mind about the baby. "Adam, I thought you love me-"

"JUST GET OUT FROM MY ROOM!" Adam shouted.

Everything seems to come into a halt and the silence is killing the both of us alive.

I looked at Adam straight in the eyes. This situation leave me in a vulnerable state but I won't let Adam have the satisfaction of seeing that on me.

I walked past Adam and get out from his room. I ran to get away from his house as far as I can. I walk home alone while crying. I have no one else to go to.

How am I going to raise this child on my own? And what about dad? These thoughts kept running through my head as I arrived home.

Being the stupid, young teenage girl that I am, I made the most stupidest decision in my life that actually sounded like the only possible solution to my problem at the time.

I went into my room and packed my clothes and other important and memorable things of mine. I know it sounded foolish that I decided to run away. Me being young and alone, I have not much people to look up to and it leads me to make such mistakes most of the time.

Dad would be ashamed if anyone finds out that his daughter is pregnant while still in high school. I won't let him go through that because of me. And I definitely don't want him struggling to find extra money to feed my baby. We barely even have money to feed ourselves. Maybe after I left, his life would be easier. He don't have to worry about me.

Before I left, I wrote a note for my dad. At least he deserves to know why I left the house.

Dad,

I'm really sorry I didn't tell you this earlier but I'm pregnant. We barely even have money to stay alive so I figured out that it would be best if I go. I'll try to raise this baby on my own, you don't have to be worried. It's not your fault that this happened. You're not a bad dad, I'm the bad one. I'm sorry I couldn't be a perfect daughter for you and mom. I'll come back when I'm ready. Please take a good care of yourself, I love you so so much.

Your daughter, Jane

Being 18 and pregnant, I feel so scared. At a young age, running away sounded like the best idea to solve my problem. Away from my dad, my only family. Away from my home, my childhood memories.

Away from Adam, the guy that broke me. Away from shame and guilt.

I thought when I ran away from home, I could run away from all my regrets and mistakes. But I was wrong, because back then I was only 18. I was still a young, clueless, and unemployed girl and still very much pregnant with no home.

I know I would probably regret it one day, but that day is not today.

-----

please VOTE, COMMENT AND FOLLOW!

Chapter 1

I force my two wobbly legs to keep walking. Only 3 minutes until I get to my apartment. My legs are super tired today, results of pole dancing for 2 hours. For someone who is only 21 years old, I'm not supposed to be this tired but working as a pole dancer really has it cons. It's not like I choose to have this life. I only do this to support my son and me.

People will definitely judge my current career but I have my own reason on why I choose to be a pole dancer. Firstly because I just love dancing in general. When I was a kid I used to dream to be a dancer when I grow up. Unfortunately, my dream can only stay a dream.

But since Danny's pub is looking for a new dancer, I mean pole dancer, so I thought why not. And the pay was also good. Or maybe the pay was high only because Danny knows my condition and he did it out of pity. Either way I'm still happy with how my life turns out right now even though it is not as flourishing as other people but I take what I can get for me and my son.

After I left home, I can't further my study in University because I have no money and I don't have any acquaintance that could help me to get a scholarship. Besides, having to take care of a baby with me while I'm busy studying during the day is definitely not gonna work for me. Unlike working in Danny's pub which is at night so I have more time during the day to spend with my son. Such a shame my smart brain won't be so useful anymore. So there goes my dream to be a Uni student.

Being 18 back then while having a baby with no working experience or any certificate from a Uni was hard for me. I can't get better jobs but I have to keep trying to feed my small family.

Fast forward now here I am working as a pole dancer because that's one of the easiest way to get money fast and doesn't need any requirements such as degree. Also the pub that I am working at was owned by a friend of mine, Danny.

I want to thank whoever is above for sending Danny my way. He has been helping me since the day we first met. Danny has been the best helpful big brother that I have never had.

In my weak state, Danny was the one to help me, provided me with a place to stay, and help me financially during my pregnancy. Though sometimes Danny could be really cocky and annoying but he is seriously the sweetest guy ever.

After my pregnancy, Danny offered me to work at his pub, Foster House. No, it is not the typical club like you thought. Danny has opened it for a music, performance and arts venue, and pub.

Honestly, I don't like being a pole dancer. I feel like I am one of those sluts or a cheap woman. But I love to dance. It is one of the things that I am passionate about. So being a pole dancer is not that bad after I did a few tries. It was just like dancing but with... a pole, obviously.

When I finally arrived at my apartment, I open the door slowly, afraid to wake up my baby who's probably sleeping since it's 12:25 am already.

I saw Mary, the babysitter, cleaning the counter at the kitchen. Mary is quite old, 52 actually, and I always told her not to clean my apartment but just take care of my son because I don't want to tire her out. But she insisted to help me. She doesn't even ask for extra pay. She knows what my job is and how do I end up here so she insisted to help me.

I'm so thankful to know these nice people still exist in our world. I wish more people could be generous and kind like Danny and Mary.

I already think Mary as my own mother. She cares about me and loves my son so much. She always said that one day someone will come along to take away my burden and shower me and my son with love. I just laughed it away knowing that no man would want a pole dancer with a baby as their wife.

"Mary, you don't have to clean the counter for me. I told you before, all you had to do is just babysit Noah for me." I said, looking at Mary with a frown.

Mary looks at me with a warm smile. "Oh Jane, stop nagging, and you know I do this because I want to right? You work hard already. You won't have time to clean your apartment so let me do it."

She's right. It's pointless to even fight her anymore. She would still do it anyway.

"Thank you, Mary. I owe you so much with all the things you've done for me. Thanks for babysit Noah today, here's your pay." I said as I lend her the money.

"Anything for you my dear. And thank you. I'll be going home now. See you again, Jane." Mary takes her purse and put on her maroon cardigan. She wave at me as she walked out of the door.

I went into my room and find my 3 years old baby boy, sleeping soundly on my bed.

Seeing Noah is always my favorite part of the day. Looking at his face always brings me peace. He has a dimple on his right cheek, just like Adam. Everyday as Noah grows up, he looks a little bit more like his father.

I'm still sad and hurt that me and Adam have to broke things off between us but that was 3 years ago and now I have moved on.

I used to think about abortion but then again, I thought, the baby is the only precious thing that Adam ever gave to me. So I kept the baby.

And it was the best decision I have ever made.

Fast forward to this day, Noah is 3 years old, as strong and healthy as a 3-year-old could be. I'm glad I kept him in the first place and didn't go with my plan of abortion.

After I was done taking a shower and changed into my pajamas, I get in the bed and crawl over to get closer to my baby. Just as I lay my head on the pillow with my arms around Noah, I immediately fall into a deep sleep.

-

The next morning, I woke up early with Noah. It's 8 am and I was preparing breakfast for Noah and me.

Noah have cereal and milk for breakfast while I'm having a burnt toast with jam.

"Mommy, you don't go to work today?" Noah asked me while his mouth is still full with cereals.

"Of course I have to go to work honey, but I don't have to go not until 8 pm, remember?" I asked him.

"Oh. Yes mommy!"

I look at him with an adoring smile. I work almost everyday except for Saturday. I miss spending time with Noah. But luckily I don't have to go to work until 8 pm. So I do have some time to spend with my baby then.

After we finished having breakfast, Noah sat on the floor and play with his toys. I sit on the two seater sofa and try to find something to watch on the TV. Suddenly, I notice a newspaper that I bought last night. I pick up the newspaper and read it.

'CEO OF THE W.W INC. , WILLIAM WINSTON, WAS SEEN LEAVING A HOTEL WITH YET ANOTHER WOMAN. DID HE FINALLY FOUND THE RIGHT ONE OR IS THIS

JUST ANOTHER ADDITION TO HIS LONG LIST OF GIRL-FRIENDS?'

Why does a love life of this CEO guy has to be on the front-page of the newspaper? Who even bother to know about his love life and who he sleeps with?

When the media has nothing interesting to write so they take this CEO guy as the victim to be their headline. Poor guy.

Everyone knows William Winston though. He's one of the richest and youngest CEO in the US. He's only 25 but managed to handle such a big company such as W.W Inc. Well, that company belongs to his family so of course being the heir of the Winston family, he has to take over the company himself.

William is always the main attraction to women. Even older women. You can never missed his toned abs and strong jaw. He's also very tall. It makes him look even more hot. At least that's what other people say. I don't really take notes about this guy. He's just another young man spoiled with wealthy and power. I also heard that he didn't do relationship.

I close the newspaper not wanting to read more about the CEO guy. It's not like he knows me anyway so why would I even bother to know about his life.

-

"Goodbye, baby. Sleep tight. I'll see you tomorrow morning okay?" I said to Noah and kiss his head.

"Alwite mommy. Night night." Noah replied.

I turn my head towards Mary and say "Goodbye, Mary. I'll see you tonight. Take a good care of my Noah!"

"Goodbye, Jane. See you. And of course I will. Now go, you're gonna be late." Mary said to me.

I close the door behind me and walk down the stairs. Ready for another night at the bar as a pole dancer.

I was wearing a coat since it's always cold at night, but underneath the coat I'm wearing a black lingerie corset dress with red heels. It's just another perfect piece of clothing to wear for a pole dancing. I bought a few sexy lingerie and lacy bras to wear during pole dancing. But it was not as revealing as you thought. They're not really my type of clothing but I have to wear them for my job's sake. Lucky me, my body is just the perfect size to be a pole dancer and anything that I wear would probably make all the man at the pub goes wild.

As I getting near the pub, I saw a black sports car parked right in front of the entrance. The sports car is definitely belongs to someone rich. But why would someone with lots of money come to this pub? This pub is not even classified as a 3 star club. Rich people don't come here. They go to a more expensive and exclusive pub with a 5 star rating.

I shook my head as I get into the pub.

As I get inside, I quickly make my way towards the back room to change my outfit which only took me a minute because I only have to get off the coat, my shirt and jeans. I already wear my 'sexy outfit' beneath all this. After that I let down my hair that has been tied into a ponytail. I put on a lipstick and some mascara with eyeliner to make myself look decent and sexy and then I'm done.

When I leave the room I immediately take my place at the podium with a pole in the middle. The podium is located in the center of the bar so when I get on the podium, almost everyone could see me.

As I take one step to the podium almost all eyes are on me already. Nice, I haven't started dancing yet but they already gave their attention to me.

Danny, the pub owner, sees me. Other than a friend and a big brother, he's also my boss so I have to listen to whatever he says. He's the one who hired me and got me accepted in this pub. I saw him went to the modern jukebox and picked a song for me to dance.

The song was on and I started to make my dance moves while shutting out the reality. I ignore all the wild eyes that wandering my body as I started dancing on the pole.

I got myself on the pole and slid down first just getting a feel for it. I go up and down on the pole which made all the man's jaw almost drop. I was able to twist myself and wrap my legs around the pole and hold myself up.

Next, I sexily pulled my hair up and let it fall around myself as I danced to the music. I pushed my bra up and my plump breasts went up as well.

I was busy dancing and making sexual movements to the pole when my eyes suddenly look straight ahead and I was met with a pair of dazzling blue eyes.

Those eyes, that face, I knew him…

Wait

Isn't that, but no way, but I'm sure that must be him!

That face belongs to no other than the famous CEO of W.W Inc. , William Winston!

What is he doing here? Shouldn't he be in a hotel, meeting CEO of other companies or something? Or at least go to a more high rated club, I thought to myself while still dancing wildly on this pole. I'm glad I didn't fall to the floor yet.

The famous CEO is looking at me with an expression that I can't explain. Why is he looking at me like that? Oh right, because I'm the only one dancing while wearing a sexy piece of outfit. He hold my gaze far longer that I'd like.

No way, he was distracting me.

I must admit, he looks really hot in that white button up shirt but he left the first three buttons open so his chest could be seen.

Oh my, I am so gonna fall from this pole if I stare at him any longer!

-----

please VOTE, COMMENT AND FOLLOW!

Chapter 2

Jane's POV

I still can't believe that William Winston went to the pub last night. To the pub that I work at, to be exact!

I actually saw him for real last night. The memory is still fresh in my mind.

And holy grail... he saw me pole dancing in just a lingerie corset!

I don't know if that was supposed to be a good first impression of me or not. But I hope for the latter.

"Mommy, mommy... MOMMY!" Noah yelled at me for the third times because I wasn't listening. Obviously.

I chuckled, "Yes love, do you need anything?" I asked Noah.

"Mommy... can we go get ice cream? I want ice cream... pwease mommy." Noah pleads at me with his cute round puppy eyes.

How can I say no to that cute face?

"Okay baby, I feel like eating ice cream too. Now let's go get ice cream!" I pick up Noah from the floor and hold him securely in my left arm. My right hand grab my purse on the coffee table and then we make our way to the front door.

We spent most of our time at the park while eating ice cream. After that, Noah went for a couple rounds on the swings with some other kids.

I also made a few conversations with the moms there. Usually I was always the youngest among the moms. Instead of getting a harsh look and rude comments from the other moms, they were actually very nice and always show support and giving me some handful mother tips. I am forever grateful to be living in such a nice society.

Later, Noah and I went home while picking up a small size of pizza along the way to bring home for dinner.

"Love, I hope you had fun today. I'm sorry baby but mommy have to go to work now. We can go eat ice cream again next time, yeah?" I told Noah.

I'm already in my another 'sexy outfit' which consist of a peach lace bra with matching panties and a peach knee socks with tiny ribbons on the top. And it was hidden underneath my long coat. When I said bra and panties, I didn't mean the kind that ladies wear everyday. This one is much more appropriate and not too revealing.

My son never knows what my work was. He only knows that I dance at uncle Danny's pub, or cafe. He's just a kid. He doesn't need to know what his mother does for a living. At least not right now.

"Okay mommy!" Noah smile at me and showing that cute dimple.

I lower myself down until I was at the same level as Noah and say, "Be a good boy tonight and then I'll buy you two ice creams! Promise mommy you'll listen to what Nanny Mary says, okay?"

Noah nods his head at me and then he gives a toothy smile at Mary.

I lean in and give a one last hug to Noah while saying, "Mommy loves you, Noah. I'll have to go now."

"Love you too mommy." Noah replied.

I stand up and about to walk out of the front door when Mary says, "Be safe, Jane."

I only smile and nod at her. I close the front door and ready for another night at the club.

Who knows, maybe William Winston will be there again. As much as my brain knows that he won't be there, deep down I really hope that he'll come again.

-

The club was not too crowded but the night is still young, most of the people would be here later.

I make my way to the podium as all eyes are on me. I look around the bar, trying to find the famous and hot CEO but he's nowhere to be seen.

He's not here.

Well, I shouldn't get my hopes too high.

After half an hour I stop dancing and take a break. The bartender gave me a drink which I'm not sure what it's called but it was pretty strong. The drink makes my throat feels burn but in a good way. I feel relieve for a second until I was met with that same pair of blue eyes from yesterday.

I was sitting on a stool at the bar while William was sitting somewhere further and more private but I can still see him.

I don't know what it is about this man but the way he looks at me makes me feel something.

After I finished my drink, I went back to the podium to start dancing again.

William keep his eyes on me all night. Somehow, in the weirdest way, I feel appreciated. Other people in the club watch me dancing while their eyes were busy focusing on all the curves on my body, but William, he stares right into my eyes, sometimes he would cut the gaze and just watch me dancing and stare at my body. But then he always keep his eyes stare right back into me as if to make sure that I look nowhere but him.

So that's the thing between us. Eye contacts. It was nothing but it means everything to me. I never adore this guy before but if you ask me again now, I would definitely say yes.

-

It has been two weeks and William Winston never seems to missed his visit at the club. I was glad though. Even though we never talk to each other but seeing him every night makes me feel happy and I dance much more wild on the pole, maybe because I was too excited, or maybe I just want to get his attention. Definitely the latter.

Tonight has been the same as usual. He would sit at his usual seat, which is actually the best seat in the pub because he can see me clearly from his place and so do I.

Every night I wait for him to approach me and talk to me but he never did. I always thought there might be something between us because he always keep his eyes on me and he has that look that screams I want you. But who am I kidding? Why would he talk to me? I'm just a pole dancer and not forget to mention I'm a single mother too while he is the young, hot and rich CEO that every girl wants.

As usual, I make my way to the podium to start dancing.

My hand wrapped tight around the sweaty pole, lifting my body up and making a small simple twirl, trying to hide the yawn that was ready to escape my lips during the act.

The music was blasting loud in the small area of the club, the crowd hollering over me while some other people are swinging their hips to the beat of the music. I also noticed one lady grabbed a chair and placed a male visitor, or maybe his boyfriend, on top of it. The lady give his boyfriend a lap dance while I was still dancing on this pole.

Great, now we have two dancers in the house! At least I'm not the only one getting wild tonight.

I had been standing on this podium for almost two hours now, my dancing becoming less and less erotic around the pole. I knew Danny was watching me but doing the same thing for hours would lead to boredom. Though I always preferred to be on the podium, it meant less attention from the guests and I wouldn't have to dedicate myself

100% to the audience. On this small podium, I did have some control over myself.

But tonight, I want to do something new. I'm tired of the same routine everyday. Tonight, I will make sure William talk to me. I don't want to keep pretending like there's nothing between us because by the way he looks at me, I know damn well he wants to get to know me too. I know having a one night stand with me must have crossed his mind once or twice. But of course I would never give myself to him for a one night stand just because he's hot and a rich CEO. Tonight, I'm gonna dance on this pole as wild as I can and as sexy as I can be. I'm gonna test his limit. I'm going to seduce him.

He always made sure to have an eye on me, no matter where he was sitting whether he was on his usual seat, leaning on the wall at the corner or drinking at the bar. Somehow his eyes always locked on mine and when he would walk pass my podium, he will wink at me.

It was almost like work was getting bored without him. Doing my dances was always something I found entertaining but it wasn't as tempting when William wasn't there to keep an eye on me.

Tonight, when I danced it wasn't for the few guys sitting in the red velvet booths. It was all for William, and I knew I was teasing him with a smirk plastered on my lips.

William give me his famous smirk, telling me that he knows what I'm doing or what I'm trying to do. It's obvious that I turn him on. My thought was right when I saw the bulge growing on his pants.

It's almost midnight but William still haven't make a move on me. Yet.

After a while, I have stopped dancing and I make my way back to the back room to change. After I was done changing I walk myself out of the pub to go home.

I don't see William anywhere. Maybe he is already on his way to the hotel to have a nice sex with some girl to solve his problem that I caused. Typical William.

I put on my coat and started my way towards my apartment, my head bowed against the wind.

I'd only gone a couple of blocks when a car pulled up alongside me. The passenger window lowered, the person in the car ducked to catch my eyes. That's when I see the familiar blue eyes.

William Winston!

"Jane is it? Come on get in, I'll drive you home." William said.

Cars honked behind him. Without a care, he just ignored them.

Not wanting the other drivers to be mad so I kept walking, I pushed my hands deep in my pockets. But William kept rolling slowly along with me.

"What? You didn't trust me? I know you know that I'm the famous William Winston. I'm the CEO of W.W Inc. Don't be shy now. Come, I'll get you home babe. You're not gonna walk in the rain aren't you? It's fine honey, you know you can trust me." He said again.

I stopped and looked at him. Cars were still honking. I can also heard someone yelled. I looked up at the night sky and it does looks like it's going to rain soon. And I don't have my umbrella with me tonight.

I sighed as I saw William leaned over and opened the door to the passenger seat.

"Just get in, okay? It's already raining. You don't want to catch a cold, right?"

Seeing that the cars behind were honking like crazy and the windy weather is getting colder, I make my way to his car and get in.

I was cold. And wet.

The heater in his car was working well. It's a freaking expensive car of course the heater works well you idiot. He angled all the vents toward me.

"Thank you, but you don't have to do that. I can just walk home." I spoke without looking at him, my purse cradled in my lap.

He looked at me with an amusing smile, "Are you serious? So you just gonna walk home alone in midnight even if it is raining too?"

I just shrugged.

He chuckled, "You're unbelievable."

I can't seem to focus on whatever he says, not because I was sitting beside a hot guy, but because I was still cold, and now I'm shivering.

William looked at me again and realized that I was still cold.

"This thing has heated seats, you know. They're great. You'll feel it in a minute, even through your coat." He told me.

I just nod my head and said nothing.

He can sense that I'm nervous so he tried to make a conversation with me to make it less awkward.

"Please put on your seat belt." Wow, nice way to start a conversation William. That's when I actually looked at him. This time, he wasn't on his usual seat in the pub or at the bar. He was right beside me. And I'm not on the podium dancing, I'm in his car.

His face is much more closer now. I can see his handsome face looking back at me. I didn't do anything or said anything. I just stared on his face.

Stop admiring over him, Jane. Have control over yourself for god sake.

He does have a very handsome face. My thighs clenched together trying to get some relieve. Damn this man sure knows how to make any women, even the virgin, to fantasize some really, really dirty things that he could do with that mouth, body, fing-

"Jane? Hello?" William snape me out of my dirty imagination.

When he realized I won't respond, he leaned over me to put on the seat belt on me. When he did that, I swear I'm about to passed out. His face was so close to me. God damn it. I can smell his cologne when he was this close to me. Fucking hell. I'm only getting wetter now.

"There you go. And stop staring at me, I know no women can't resist me. You don't have to make it obvious though." He smirked at me.

Damn this man sure has his ego as high as Mount Fuji.

He might be hot and rich but his ego will get him nowhere. Decided to ignore his cocky attitude I just tell him where I live.

"Okay, we'll be there in a minute. So, you are Jane right? The pole dancer at the club?" He asked me.

I cringed when he said pole dancer. I might be a pole dancer but I don't like to talk about it outside the pub or if I'm not working at the moment.

Suddenly I realized something.

He knows my name.

I turned to look at him, "How did you know my name? I never told you and we never talk."

He just looked at me and chuckled, "I have my way, babe."

I admit, butterflies erupt in my stomach the moment I heard him called me babe. But I show no emotion and raised my eyebrows to him. I want a real and complete answer.

"Fine, Danny told me. He's your boss, right? He also told me that you were known as Sexy J at the club." He gave me that famous smirk again.

Yes, I am also known as Sexy J. A nickname given by Danny himself. Everyone at the club and most of our regular visitors and customers called me Sexy J. I don't really like the nickname given to me, but after a while, I get used to it. Danny said the name suits me since I do have a really sexy body. His words, not mine.

"Only people at the club call me Sexy J. Please, just call me Jane." I told William.

"Jane...?"

"Jane Rosenfeld."

William smile with satisfaction, "Ahh, what a beautiful name for such a beautiful lady."

William looked at me with a genuine smile but I realized that must have been one of his way to get into my pants. As much as I want to be taken by him, I still refused to sleep with him. I'm not like other women. I might be a pole dancer but I don't sleep around easily. In fact, I haven't get laid since the last time I did it with Adam.

"I saw you were looking at me back there in the club. Why? And why do you start to make a move now? Trying to drive me home just to get into my pants? Wow, smooth William, very smooth." I looked at him while giving him an angry glance.

"Wow Sexy J, you sure could be blunt and straight to the point sometimes yeah?" He give me that damn smirk again.

Oh god that smirk makes him look sexy. I'm so done.

"Don't call me that and no I'm not blunt. I'm just telling the truth."

I don't like people calling me Sexy J when I'm outside the pub but somehow the way he calls me that gives me chills. It's like a turn on for me. He makes that name sounds sexy when hearing him say it.

"Alright, Jane. Okay so what do you want to talk about?" He asked me.

Is he even serious? He wants to have a casual talk with me?

God this man is driving me crazy. Why does the drive took so long. Ugh. I just want to go home already and sleep with my baby. Oh my baby, Noah...

"Cut the crap William. I know who you are. You don't just have casual talk with any women. Ever. So tell me, what do you want?" I asked him. Okay, maybe I could be a bit blunt sometimes.

"You want me to tell the truth or a lie?" He asked me with a serious face.

Did he really just asked me that? Wow, what kind of question is that?

"The truth of course." I replied.

William slowed down the car and parked alongside the road. He turns to look at me in the eyes.

"You want the truth? Fine, here's the fucking truth. The first time I saw you on that pub, pole dancing like the slut you are makes me want you. But somehow I don't think I can just take you and fuck you then leave. So I wait and tried to have some self control which I never done before and it was so fucking hard because seeing you dancing on that podium only makes me hard. So hard. But you have no idea, do you? Or maybe you do because the way you looked at me I can tell that you want me as bad as I want you."

He stopped and looked around then he turned off the headlights. He turned his gaze to me again. This time I can see something different on his eyes. His dazzling blue eyes turned into a darker shade of blue. Then I realized, it's the look of lust.

"Now I'm going to tell you what I want. I want you. Each night seeing you dancing on that pole makes me crazy Jane, crazy! I can't help it. I want you! All I'm asking is just a one night together and then we could forget each other. Easy."

Of course, knowing him, all he want is just a one nice fuck and then that's it. And of course I would say no. But first, I want to know why he only said this now? Why not earlier?

"Why you tell me now? Why not earlier? You never tried to talk to me. You could have just ask me for my name instead of asking Danny."

"Danny told me about you. He said you could be wild and exotic in the pub and on the podium, but that's not really you. You rarely talk to anyone and he never saw you being intimate with anyone since you first started working there. He confirmed my thoughts about you. You are different. That's why I took some time to get to you, I want to wait a little longer but tonight I just can't. You seemed different at the club tonight. As if you were trying to lure me in. I can't help it, Jane. You looked so fucking sexy tonight, baby, and I love that. I want that. I want you."

I listened to every single words he said. Some of them makes me hot and bothered. Some makes me want to slap him. Hard.

I don't know what to say. I didn't know that I could make him want me that bad. I almost laugh at that thought because how can a hot CEO like William would want someone like me? Life sure is unpredictable sometimes.

Realizing that I'm not gonna say anything, William starts his car and drive again. We sat in silence throughout the drive to my apartment. He didn't even look at me.

Is he mad?

Why would he be mad?

But if this is how he looks like whenever he's mad then I should always make him mad because he sure does looks hot when he's mad.

Perks of being William Winston, you will always looks hot even when you're mad.

I can already see my apartment through the car's window. I still haven't said anything to him.

I take off my seat belt. "Thank you."

"Jane, please... just one night. That's all I'm asking." William asked me.

Damn it, he said please.

I didn't know that the word 'please' exists in his world. I also didn't see him as someone who will beg woman to sleep with him.

As if he read my mind he said, "I never beg or chase after a girl, Jane. Women always throw themselves at me. But you, you are different. I don't know what it is about you but I have the urge to have you. So bad. I just need to have you. I want you."

I looked at him one last time before I get out from the car. I ducked my head to look at him from outside the car.

"I'm not like other women you slept with. I don't want to be like one of them." I told him. "Goodnight Mr. Winston."

I closed the passenger door and walked straight ahead to get into my apartment.

I want to see Noah. I miss my baby.

I only talked to William once but I miss him more already.

His words echoed in my head.

"I want you"

Maybe a one night with William wouldn't be so bad.

Just spend one night with him and then we go back to normal.

Easy, right?

I wrote 3K+ words for this chapter. I hope it's not too long for you to read. Let me know if you preferred long update or short update!

please VOTE, COMMENT AND FOLLOW!

Chapter 3

Hi guys! So I know this story is supposed to be all romance between Jane and William but that's not the only thing I want to focus on this book, I also want to show the love of a single mother towards her child who works hard to make sure her child could live the life they deserve.

This chapter contains more Jane and Noah's scene so you could see the mother-son bond between them.

Happy reading!

Jane's POV

I woke up this morning with one thing on my mind. No scratch that, it's actually one person in my mind. And that person is no other than William Winston.

I still can't believe that I talked to William. It's the famous William Winston we're talking about here!

He had occupied my mind since last night. I can't even sleep properly. Thank god it's Saturday so I don't have to go to work and I don't have to see William. At least I could get a decent sleep tonight.

I shouldn't be thinking about William. Today I'm gonna give all my attention to Noah instead of stressing over that cocky CEO.

Noah is still sleeping soundly beside me. I hopped out of bed and went to the bathroom to wash my face. After that I went to the kitchen to prepare some breakfast for Noah and I.

I was slavering away over the frying pan making pancakes that I didn't notice Noah had crept into the kitchen.

"Hey, morning baby." I walked over to Noah and kiss him on the forehead.

Noah rubbed his eyes sleepily like a kitten, "Morning, mommy."

"I'm making pancakes for breakfast! Do you want chocolate or fruits to eat with your pancakes?"

"Chocolate." Noah replied, eyes closing a little.

I chuckled, looking at my baby. He almost doze of again. "Okay, baby. Coming right up!"

After we had breakfast, I saw Noah was busy coloring in front of the TV. The TV was still on, showing some breakfast morning show.

I went over to Noah and sit beside him. He looked up at me and show me his coloring book.

"Mommy, look! Nanny Mary bought me this coloring book! She even bought me color pencils. She said I can color on this book when you're busy."

Don't get me wrong but I get a bit disappointed at his words.

First, because Mary is the one who has to buy him a coloring book and color pencils. I'm supposed to buy that for him but I didn't. Not because I don't want to but I have to save the money that I have for the rent, bills and groceries. The last time I bought something for Noah was 2 months ago. I bought him a play fishing set. That was the cheapest toy I could get at a convenience store.

Second, it feels like I'm not always at home anymore. Am I always busy? Maybe I don't give much attention to Noah. I feel bad for him and I hate myself for that. He needs to feel appreciated and loved. And I do love him, so much. He's my everything. My lifeline.

Anyhow, I'm glad Mary bought him the coloring book and color pencils. A 3 year old like Noah should start learning how to color, count and spell. It's good to see him develop and getting smarter. He's gonna be a smart kid one day and live a much better life.

"You're really good at coloring, Noah. You should do it more. I will buy you another coloring book next time okay?" I told him.

"Okay mommy!" Noah give me his toothy smile.

-

There's no good show to watch on the TV anymore. I've been watching TV since Noah went to the bedroom to play with his toys.

I realized that even on Saturday I barely spend my time with Noah. I should do something to make him happy. He must be bored playing in the room with his same old toys all day.

I went to the bedroom and saw Noah was playing with his mini figure toys on the bed. I get on the bed and scoot closer to him.

"Hey, baby. It's Saturday and do you know what it means?" I asked Noah who was looking at me curiously.

"You didn't have to work today!" Noah exclaimed.

"Yes love but that's not the only thing. Today we're going out! I'm gonna take you to the park so you could have some playtime and maybe make friends."

"Yay! I want to go to the park. When are we going mommy?" Noah asked me eagerly. I can see he's already excited to go out. It feels good to see him happy.

"We're going right now! Now go and change while I go prepare some biscuits and a juice to bring with us to the park."

"Okay mommy!" Noah smiled and hurriedly went up to get ready.

I was in the kitchen when I looked up and saw my 3 years old son, Noah, dressed and ready for our day at the park, not counting the fact that his shoes were on the wrong feet.

I chuckled as my little son waddled over, struggling to stay up because of his mixed up shoes. I got up from the dining chair and met Noah at the doorway, scooping him up in my arms and carrying him over to the table.

"You look cute, sweetie. But there's one thing left to do before we go. You don't want to trip yourself while playing. Right, baby?" I sat down with Noah in my lap and untied the knots he'd put in his shoe strings and switched them to the proper feet, tying them tight for him.

"And now you're ready to go!" I said happily.

Noah was just incredibly excited to go play at the park. I took his hand and helped him down off my lap. Noah rambled on as I let him drag me along behind him.

"And we're gonna ride the slide, and you can push me really high on the swings!" Noah chatted all the way to the park.

It was fairly busy this time of day, and I could already feel the eyes on me from around the park. I got out of the bus and helped Noah get out, holding his hand as he hurriedly pulled me along.

"Let's go!" Noah squealed, giving up on waiting for me and letting go so he could run off to the playground.

I chuckled and let him play, finding a bench to myself and bringing out my phone. I admit, I wasn't very good at this whole single mom thing, but I was trying my best. I could tell, just from the look on Noah's face, how much fun Noah was having, and that was what really mattered to me.

After a while, I heard a yelp and looked up. My head whipped around and I immediately stuffing my phone in my bag. Noah had fallen off the monkey bars and was clutching his knee in tears.

"Noah!" I screamed.

I jogged over to Noah and knelt down beside him. "Are you all right sweetie?"

Noah looked up at me through his tears and uncovered his knee for me to see. It was scraped up pretty badly and was getting blood all over the end of his shorts. "I hurt my knee." He whimpered.

I held my arms out to him. He reached up and took my arms, letting me pick him. I scooped him up in my arms and carried him over to the swings, picking up my bag over my shoulder quickly and asking him, "Does it hurt? It's okay, sweetie. Let's go home and get you cleaned up, yeah?"

Noah has tears all over his face. I hate seeing him cry. He rarely cry before, he was such a good boy.

"It's okay baby, don't cry. Mommy's got you now." I hold him tight in my arms and I don't wanna let go, ever.

Once at home, I pulled some bandage and antiseptic out of my first aid kit. I took out a cotton pad and started dabbing antiseptic along Noah's knee.

He winced and let out another whimper.

"I'm sorry sweetie, but when I finish how about I get you some lollipops, okay?"

It's already evening when we got home. Taking a public bus really did took a lot of your time.

I smiled as I laid Noah down in bed and pulled the covers up over Noah's shoulders. "Now, get some sleep, baby. I love you, bud."

"I love you too, mommy." Noah yawned at me, whining and reaching for my arm as I stood up.

"Stay with me." Noah requested, his eyes drooping already.

I smiled and looked at the clock. I thought about watching TV after putting Noah to sleep but seeing him like this makes my heart melt. What's a better thing to do than being with your son, right? I looked at Noah again and nodded.

"Of course, baby. Just let me turn off the light." I whispered, standing and heading to the light switch. I turned off the light and then climbed into bed beside Noah.

"Now just close your eyes and get to sleep, little one." I kissed Noah's hair and smiled as the boy snuggled closer.

Moments like this are my favorite. Just being close with my boy, Noah. No interruption or work can separate us.

I'm glad that Noah is still happy that we went to the park today even though he scrapped his knee. He's such a strong little boy. My little hero. I'll do anything for him. He deserves every happiness in the world.

"I love you my little hero." I whispered slowly into his ear.

-

The next day, when I arrived at the pub I know that he's here already. William. I saw his car parked in front of the pub.

I tried so hard not to think about him. And Noah was being a really good distraction for me not to think about the cocky-yet-so-fucking-hot man. But after a day not seeing him makes me feel like I'm missing something. Missing him. I missed his wandering blue eyes that always had his gaze on me and my body.

Tonight when I was on my way to work, I can already felt the excitement of seeing him again.

The bass throbbed throughout the club, enticing seductive grinds from my hips. I slither against the pole, sliding up and down, bending backwards to see the reactions from the sweaty bodies on the small dance floor. Most were wrapped up, literally, in their partners, but that one, with the blue eyes, dirty blonde hair... he's watching right into me. I can see the hunger in his eyes from across the room. I watch him as his eyes slide from mine, down my body, so slowly... his tongue peeks out to swipe across his bottom lip.

Damn. I'd like to run my tongue across that lip.

-----

please VOTE, COMMENT AND FOLLOW!

Chapter 4

WARNING: The following chapter may contain mature content and strong language which may be offensive and/or inappropriate for some readers.

Jane's POV

As I step through the back room, a warm hand touches my shoulder. I slowly turn my head and my blue eyes, blonde haired god is standing there, a sexy smile on his face.

Smirking, I take his hand and lead him back to the back room. I lock the door behind us. He moves farther into the room, watching me. I lean back against the door, letting my eyes run slowly down his body, taking close note of the lean muscles in his chest, leading down to a narrow waist.

"So it's a yes then? For a one night together?" William asked me with an amusing smile.

"Just one night and that's all, right?" I looked into his eyes and then return to look at his body.

"Yep, just one night baby. Only tonight. That's all I'm asking." He winked at me.

This is it. I can't back out now. I can't believe I give in so easily. We're gonna do this. This will be the first time I sleep with someone after Adam. I try to block everything out. I try not to think about Noah at home, probably sleeping. Now, I'm just gonna focus on this man in front of me.

"I'm usually the man in action, babe. I'm always the one in charge. But tonight, I want to see that Sexy J inside you. Bring her out, come on. You own me tonight, baby." William told me with lust in his voice.

That's it. He's giving me the permission to make the first move. I'm not really an expert in bed but I'm not that stupid. Tonight, I'm not a Jane. Say hello to Sexy J.

Licking my lips as I get to his belt, I glance up at him to see him giving me the once over as well. The bulge in his jeans is impressive. I want to taste him. Moaning, I close my eyes for a minute. I feel his warm breath on my face and open my eyes to find him staring at me and moving his lips to mine.

His lips molding to mine. Slowly, sliding his tongue across my bottom lip, he ask for more. I parts my lips, his tongue stroking mine, then gently exploring my mouth. Damn. He tastes so good.

I haven't been intimate with anyone since Adam and god... how much have I been missing out? I miss having someone so close to me like this. Not the cuddle-snuggle-in-bed-with Noah kind of close but the kissing and touching kind of company I'm talking about here.

My hands slide from his shoulders, slowly downward. Stroking his chest, teasing along the ridges of his muscles lightly with my blunt nails. I reach for the top button of his shirt, my eyes asking permission. He nods. I kiss each revealed patch of skin as I undo the buttons, one by one.

His lips move from mine to nibble at my earlobe and slowly work their way down my neck. His breath is hot against my skin, eliciting a soft moan from me. Sliding my hands under his shirt, I work it off his broad shoulders and down his arms.

His hips begin to grind against my throbbing area. I press closer to him, he groans, pushing harder against me.

Slipping my fingers under the waistband of his suit pants and boxers, I wrap my hand around his length. Peering up at him through my lashes, I see his head fall back, mouth open, softly moaning as his hips push himself into my hand. My other hand eases up to undo his pants as I continue to stroke him. I slide them down and get a good look, it was heavy with need and gently throbbing.

Looking up at him through my lashes, I see him watching me, eyes hooded and dark. His hands caress my scalp, gently wrapping his fingers in my hair. He might be the dominant one but his move right now say otherwise. He's not controlling, but appreciating.

Taking him all the way into my mouth, I flatten my tongue and suck him in as deep as I can, feeling him hit the back of my throat. His hips jerk forward, sliding him into my throat. I swallow around him, then slide him back out, hollowing my cheeks as I suck, tongue dancing around his length.

"Fuck" his cursed came out in a whisper.

"You're so fucking good with your mouth, baby." He shudders, then gently pulls me off him. I look at him questioningly. Smiling at me, he takes my hand, leading me to the chaise lounge in the corner.

Quickly, he removes my g-string, he gropes my breast for a minute. Damn, his hand feels good. Pushing me down on the chaise, he lies next to me, pulling me in for a passionate kiss.

As his head pulls slowly back off, he gently runs his teeth along my body, eliciting groans from deep in my chest. My hips begin to jerk erratically.

The night went on with more groans and moans from William and me. I'm not sure if I'm gonna regret this later, but it's too late to back off now. So tonight, I surrender myself to the CEO himself.

-

The next morning, I woke up alone on the chaise with a light sheet draped across me. He's gone. I knew this is bound to happen but only now I feel the loss. I clean up, get on my clothes for the trip home alone.

As I walked out from the back room, I saw Danny looking at me with a smirk on his face.

"Jane, Jane, Sexy J... I always knew you had it in you. You even managed to tame the wild tiger yourself." Danny said.

I choose to ignore him. His words makes me feel like a bad girl.

I sighed. "Please Danny, I don't want to talk about it. Not now."

"Okay, sorry." Danny held his hands up in surrender. "Anyway, from now on I'll double up your pay. Mr. Winston's order. That man is lucky, you sure are a good lay huh, because of you, he wants me to pay you double." Danny said with a not so satisfied tone.

"What? He asked you to pay me double and you just gonna follow his order? I mean, I know he's a powerful man but not so powerful that even anyone out of his building would take order from him." I gave Danny my tired face. I just want to go home already.

"Please, Danny. I'm tired and I want to go home. You don't have to increase my pay. My current pay is enough."

Honestly, I'm not mad that he is taking order from William. But I'm just mad and annoyed that William asked Danny to do that.

Who the hell does he think he is?

A rich CEO, right.

But that doesn't mean he could order people around. And he can't expect me to accept the extra pay. So, just because we had sex last night it doesn't mean he should pay me back with money. I don't want his money!

"Just take it, Jane. William, that man could make this club closed down. If that happens, my life would be screwed and you will lost your job." Danny told me.

I don't want to think about this. Damn William. I just give myself to him last night and today I still have to face another crap shit from him. Why can't he just leave me alone?

"Fine." I said to Danny and walked out of the club.

Before I reached for the door I heard Danny yelled, "Hey, be careful out there. Just come by later with Noah and get some coffee. Oh and call me if you need anything."

I gave him a thumbs up and slowly walked out of the pub. In the morning, the pub turns into something more like a cafe or diner and the morning coffee can always make you feel like home.

I make my way home slowly. My mind keep thinking about last night. His hands felt so warm when he touched me, his lips felt so soft when he kissed me, his thrust was so deep I think I almost passed out last night.

It's like 7 in the morning when I arrived at my apartment.

As I open my front door, I saw Mary and Noah were sleeping on the couch. Mary is awake from her sleep and immediately see me approaching her.

"Jane! You're home and safe! God, I was worried about you. I called you last night but you didn't pick up. Where have you been?" Mary looked at me with a worried face. I feel bad for not calling her last night.

"I'm really sorry, Mary. My shift got extended so I have to work extra hours. The pub was pretty loud so I must have not heard when you called me." I lied, but the latter was true though. The pub was indeed a little loud last night.

"Oh dear, I was really worried. Noah went to sleep late last night. He wants to wait for you, and we ended up sleeping on the couch." Mary explained.

I looked at Noah then return my gaze to Mary. "I'm sorry. But thank you for looking out after him."

BEAUTIFUL DISASTER

I open my purse and pulled out some money. "Here's your pay. I'll give you extra since you've been looking after him for the whole night."

Mary sighed, "Jane, it's my job to look after him. You don't have to pay me this much, you need it yourself."

"It's okay, Mary. Danny has doubled my salary. It'll be enough for me to pay you extra too." I handed the money to her again. This time, she took it.

"Thank you, Jane. I guess I should leave now. My husband must be waiting for me at home. I have to prepare his breakfast." Mary said, chuckling.

Mary put on her usual maroon cardigan and ready to leave.

"Thank you, Mary. I'm really sorry for causing any trouble." I told her.

Mary looked at me with a warm smile, "It's all good dear. I'm leaving now. Goodbye."

Mary give Noah a kiss on his head and then wave at me before she leave through the front door.

I went to the couch and snuggle closer to Noah. I need some sleep to clear my mind from last night's memory.

I feel uneasy when I'm about to post this chapter. Anyway feel free to leave comments or suggestions!

please VOTE, COMMENT AND FOLLOW!

Chapter 5

William's POV

I have dated many attractive women. Most of them are models and celebrities. The relationship usually lasted only for days or weeks. None of them worth my time anyway but it's good to always have them available for a nice fuck. I get bored easily so that's why the relationship never lasted more than a month.

I haven't found someone that can truly makes me feel like really in love and wants to settle down. My definition of love was just another word of lust and game.

When I first saw Jane, I just knew she was different. On the first night seeing her, I was determined she would come and seduce me. But no, it didn't happened. I guess she was not interested in me or just playing hard to get. But no women can resists me so it's probably the latter.

I still remember when I asked Danny about her. And my guess was right, she was different.

After that one night with her, I really thought I'm already over her. I really thought that I can finally forget all about her. Her eyes, her smile, her body... so sexy, very seductive.

I was completely wrong. I'm still not over her. It only makes it worse, I want her more.

Now that I already have a taste of her, I can't help but want more.

Fuck, what is happening to me.

-

Jane's POV

Tonight, I'm wearing a matching white rhinestone bra and panties with white high knee socks. This rhinestone bra and panties are my favorite. Even though I'm not really into this kind of outfit, if it's not for work, but I always love wearing this rhinestone set because it gives the sophisticated and glamour look on me.

I let down my dark brown wavy hair and put on a red lipstick. I look into the mirror in the back room and make sure I look good before I go out.

I'm back to my usual routine. I went to the pub, get changed on the back room, dance on the podium for hours, have a drink, and then went home. No more distraction from a certain CEO.

It's been a while since I last saw William, which is on the night that we spent together. I'm glad he kept his words. He didn't bother me ever since. And not to forget that my salary has been doubled, which is a bonus from sleeping with him.

But, deep in my heart, I still hope he would visit the pub again like he always did. I started to miss him.

As the night went on, I realized I've been dancing for hours and now I'm sitting at the bar and have a drink. I don't intend to get drunk so I only drink juice.

I look at the crowd who was dancing, or more like grinding, at the hardwood dance floor, mostly with their partners.

I was lost in my own thoughts that I didn't realized someone was calling my name.

I was snapped out of my gaze when looked up and saw William was standing in front of me.

He moved over and sit at the stool next to me. His gaze never leaving mine.

"How are you?" William asked casually.

So what, we're friends now?

"I'm good, as always." I replied curtly.

William only nod and he doesn't look like he's gonna say anything soon, so I asked him back the same question to avoid the awkwardness.

William looked at me for a moment before his gaze focus on the crowd, "I've been better."

That's all he said. He's strangely very quite tonight. I wonder what's wrong. Haven't found a new chick to get laid with, maybe.

"Haven't seen you in a while, I thought that maybe you wouldn't want to visit this pub anymore after that night." I said as I look at a certain couple who were grinding at each other. Lust was written all over their face. No doubt William is also watching them. The couple brought a few attention to themselves from the crowd.

"Look, I know I said that one night was all I need and then we're over, but, I can't... I don't... it's just... ugh I don't know how to say it." This is the first time I ever see him like this. So frustrated and... nervous? He's always the carefree guy and never seems to be stressed about anything, even in newspapers and magazines, his face was always seen in a smile or in that famous smirk of his.

"I'm not really a good listener but I'm willing to give it a try. So go ahead, tell me what's up. You got rejected by some chick?" I asked.

That was supposed to be sarcastic or something funny just to enlighten him. But nope, it's clearly not working. His face turned into a frown.

"Hey, I was only joking. Besides, I haven't had a casual chat with anyone lately. It's been a long time since I have someone to talk to." I told him.

It is true though. I never had any friends, only some acquaintance, but not close enough to have some casual talk on the phone. To be honest, Noah is the only person I've talked to. Besides Mary, of course. And then there's Danny, but we rarely talk since he was always busy at the pub, unless when I visit him at the pub during the day. Mostly during my working hour he only gives me some of those "Good job, today!" "That dance was amazing as always, J!" comments and sometimes asked about Noah. So yeah, it's been a long time since I had a company.

"Jane, I know you're not like other girls, but please tell me that night we spent together was good enough to convince you to spend another night with me? Because to me, that night was amazing. I would do anything to have it again." William looked at me and his tone almost sounds like he's pleading.

I was shocked. Like, literally shocked.

So he left me that night after having a night full of pleasure, he didn't said goodbye or anything. He don't even left a note. He left me, just like that. And then I was getting better at forgetting him, his eyes, his touch, after not seeing him for almost a week. But, bam! Now he's back and tell me that he wants to have sex with me again? Huh, let me guess, he couldn't find any other chick to please him tonight? I'm not that kind of woman. I'm not easily gonna give in. Not again.

So I say the first word that came into my mind.

"No"

-----

please VOTE, COMMENT AND FOLLOW!

Chapter 6

Jane's POV

"Good morning, mommy!" I heard Noah greeted me.

"Morning, my favorite boy. Mommy's making pancakes for you, baby." I told him.

"Mommy can we go out today? I want to go to the park again. Pwease?" Noah asked.

I put the pancakes on the plate and give it to Noah. "Baby, I think we should just stay home today, okay? Remember what happened the last time we went to the park? You hurt yourself, we don't want that to happen again now do we?"

"But mommy..." Noah whined.

"We can watch TV together! Or we can watch Lion King again if you want. That sounds fun, right?"

"But I want to go out. Please, mommy..." Noah give me his best puppy face. How can I say no to my baby when he's making that face?

"Fine, but finish your breakfast first and then go change." I said sternly.

"Okay mommy!" Noah smiled sheepishly, clearly satisfied that his plan is working.

-

Later, I get dressed into a dark green T-shirt and pair it with a black jeans. I grab my bag and took Noah's hand with me and lead us to the front door.

As we walked out from the apartment, I saw a familiar car parked near us.

William got out from the car and walked toward us. His outfit is more casual today, dark jeans and white T-shirt. No matter what he wears, he still look hot.

"Jane, I was about to meet you. I thought you would want to have a lunch together." William said as he approaching.

"No thanks, William. If this is your way to get me to sleep with you again then just forget it." I told William.

He was eyeing me and Noah when he said, "I didn't know you were going out. Is this your little brother?" William asked.

I was hesitated to answer him.

"Mommy, who is he?" Noah asked, walking closer to me and hiding behind my leg.

I looked at Noah and gave him a reassuring smile, "It's okay, sweetie"

"Woah, what? I'm confused. You act like he's your son or somet hing... I... what?" William is probably curious about Noah. I don't blame him, though. Anyone would have give the same reaction.

There's no point in hiding now. William might as well just know the truth about me. Maybe then he would leave me alone after knowing that I have a child.

I sighed and prepare myself for his reaction as I told him, "William, this is my son, Noah."

William gasped for a moment, looking at me with wide eyes. "Your son? You didn't tell me you have a son. I didn't know you were married... or have a boyfriend."

He looked shocked, and then his face looks like he just came up with a realization.

"Ugh, fuck. Of course you already have someone. That's why you refused to sleep with me and you never been intimate with anyone before, like Danny said. You have a boyfriend, that's why! Fuck, fuck!"

He looked very frustrated.

"Actually, William, I don't-"

"Mommy, why is he mad? I'm scared." Noah whimpered.

"Hey, shush, baby it's okay. You don't have to be scared. Mommy's here." I tried to calm Noah who looked like he was about to cry.

William sighed and looked at me, "Jane, I'm sorry. I should have know."

I turned to look at William, "William, stop it. Yes, he is my son but I don't have a boyfriend. Now if you could just leave us, please."

William was stunt, "Wait, you don't have a boyfriend? What about his father?" He asked.

"That question is a bit personal don't you think? Now if you don't mind, we have somewhere to go." I said.

I walked passed William with Noah beside me. Suddenly, I felt a hand grab my wrist. I turned my head back and look at William.

"Look, Jane, I'm sorry okay? I didn't know."

"Let go of me William." I snapped at him. "We have to go, we need to catch the bus."

William let go of my wrist slowly, "Okay, where are you going? Let me send you. Please, Jane."

"Mommy, I'm hungry." Noah whispered to me, but I'm pretty sure William could still heard him.

William leveled himself to the same height as Noah, "Hey kid, Noah is it? You hungry? C'mon, let's get a lunch. What do you want to eat?"

"No William, we can go on our own. Let's go, Noah. We'll go eat something and then I'll bring you to the park." I take Noah's hand and drag him with me as I tried to get away from William. This man annoyed me already.

"Jane, please. Let me take you and Noah to lunch and then we could talk this out." William pleaded.

"We are not going with you, William. There's nothing to talk about. Please leave us alone." I said, still walking while William was trying to stop me.

"Jane, please."

My walking comes to a halt. This man would never leave me alone until he get want he wants. I have no choice.

"Fine, William. But this doesn't mean I'm gonna sleep with you."

William smirk a little before it turns into a smile. "Right, c'mon. Get into my car."

I turned around and walk toward his car with Noah.

William looked at Noah and ask him, "So, what do you want to eat bud?"

Noah gave him a toothy smile then said, "Chicken nuggets! Lots of chicken nuggets!"

I couldn't help but smile at Noah. He looks so cute. And probably hungry too.

"Noah, where is your manners?" I gave Noah my motherly tone. Sometimes I like being a mom so just I could use that tone.

"Sorry, mommy." Noah bowed his head a little.

"That's okay, Jane. Alright, Noah. We'll go get you lots of chicken nuggets, yeah?"

"Yay!" Noah sounds very happy. I like seeing him happy like this.

Later, we found ourselves at one of the closest fast food restaurant.

Noah was eating his chicken nuggets when I told William about Adam. I never tell anyone about my past, except Mary and Danny. This is the first time I open up to someone after a while. I never trust anyone to tell them about my past, but William always got his way and get me to open up to him.

"That guy don't deserve you. How could he leave you with a baby." William said, I can feel a vortex of anger swirled inside him but he tried to still his rage.

I looked besides me, making sure that Noah is not listening to our conversation. Luckily, he was too engrossed with his chicken nuggets to even noticed his surroundings.

"William, like I said, he don't want the baby and we never plan on it anyway. It's not his fault. I was just too stupid to think he would change for me. I was too in love with him back then." I told him.

I looked at Noah again who still have his attention to the chicken nuggets. I'm glad he didn't heard us. Noah rarely ask about his father. Usually, when he started to ask about his dad I would just change the topic. Luckily, he got the message that I didn't want to talk about it and never ask again.

"But I never regret my decision to keep Noah. He's my everything. His feature did remind me of Adam sometimes but I already moved on from him so it's not a problem to me anymore. Besides, Noah might have Adam's look but not his personality. Noah is a ball of sunshine. Even at the age of 3, he's already smart enough to think like a 10-year-old. I love him with all my heart, I'll do anything for him-"

"Including you being a pole dancer." William smirk.

"Yes, including me working as a pole dancer. I told you I can't get any good jobs without a degree. I choose to do this. And I love to dance so that's not a problem." I explained.

"It must be hard trying to raise him all on your own." William said while he has his gaze on Noah.

"I admit, it is hard. I'm trying so hard to keep him happy and satisfied but I still think I failed him at some point." I confessed with a frown on my face.

To be honest, I am really insecure and always doubt myself as a mother. I was really young when I first knew I was pregnant. I struggled too much back then. But in the end, after I get to hold Noah in my hand for the first time, all the struggles are worth it.

"He looks like a happy kid. I think you did a great job as a single mother, Jane. Trust me, I'm not saying this so you would think nicely of me, I meant it Jane." William looked at me in the eyes when he said that. I don't see the cocky CEO man that I knew, this one, is another side of William Winston that I'm about to find out.

"Thank you, William." I smile genuinely. He return the smile with no doubt.

I like us like this. No cocky comments or any sexual tension floating in the air. We just had a conversation. A very deep conversation may I add. And Noah is also with us. This is new and different. A good kind of different. I really like this William.

I really like him.

"So how's the chicken nuggets, Noah? You like it?" William asked Noah.

"Thank you, uncle Will! I love it!" Noah exclaimed.

And it looks like Noah really likes him too.

After Noah finished eating his chicken nuggets, William drove us back home.

"Thank you, William. For the lunch and for sending us home. You know we could just take the bus." I told William.

"You don't have to thank me Jane. Besides, Noah looks more happy getting to ride in my car." William chuckles while looking at Noah.

Noah never actually ride in a car before. That's another thing I can't afford for him. When William asked to send us home, Noah was really happy and excited.

"Noah, do you have anything to say to uncle Will?" Yes, Noah called him uncle Will, I tried to tell him it's uncle William but William stopped me from doing so. He said he likes it when Noah calls him that. It sounds so 'natural', his word not mine.

"Thank you, uncle Will. Can you take me out again next time? Mommy rarely takes me out." Noah show his cute little pout to William.

Oh this kid.

"Noah!" I hissed.

William just chuckled, "That's okay, Jane. And of course Noah. I would take you out anytime you want me to. But if only your mom allow me to bring you guys out again."

"Mommy, pwease! Can we go out with uncle Will again? Pwease mommy, pwease?" Noah pleaded.

"Alright, alright. But only if uncle Will is not busy and not working. We don't want to bother him, honey. Uncle Will is a really busy man." I told Noah.

"Yes, okay mommy! Yay!" Noah high five William who also has a big smile on his face.

My heart warms at the sight of Noah looking happy. This is the first time William meets Noah but he already got that kid wrapped around his finger.

-

William's POV

This is the first time I met Noah but that kid already got me wrapped around his finger.

The kid is literally a ball of sunshine. I don't know why I was so keen to him, I don't even like kids before, but Noah is just different. Just like his mom. Yep, just like Jane.

That bastard Adam was such an asshole. When Jane told me about her past, about Adam, I have a sudden anger at this Adam guy. He doesn't deserve Jane, and Noah. He didn't deserve to be Jane's first. How dare he take away her pureness and then left.

Fucking asshole.

I was surprised that Jane was opening up to me. Like she said, she hasn't had a real conversation with anyone since a really long time, so of course I'll try to be the nice guy and listen to her story. Instead of feeling bored, listening to her story only makes me eager wanted to know more about her. Now this is something else.

I don't know what happened to me, but as long as Jane was fine with it, I think I'm doing okay.

What really surprised me is that my needs of wanting to sleep with her is not there at all. Well, not not at all, of course it was still there, but the feeling is not as strong as before.

Having a conversation is actually a good thing. This is actually the first time I've had an actual conversation with a woman, besides all the meetings I've been to. Jane makes me want to have a casual talk. She makes me want to listen. I was never a good listener, but for her I tried. Talking to her helped me to have some self control. Which is a good thing. I feel like a different man. Jane was changing me and she doesn't even know it. She is slowly changing my perspective of love.

Maybe real love does exist. But only if you have found the right one, because only they can show you and makes you feel what love is. Fuck, I sound like a love expert.

Maybe I don't really need to sleep with her. She's not that kind of girl so I'm not gonna treat her like that. She deserves better. Jane's already had a hard time raising Noah, I'm not that bad that I'm willing to play her like the other girls. With Jane, I'm gonna take it slow.

I don't know if I should be scared and stay away from Jane. But staying away from her is impossible when the thoughts of her filled my mind all the time. Maybe I should give whatever this thing is a chance. I should give it a try and see where it brings me.

And I hope with all my heart Jane would do the same.

-

Jane's POV

"Mommy?" Noah called out for me.

I looked at him with an adoring smile. "Yes, love?"

"Do you like uncle Will?" He asked.

I shrugged, "I don't know, baby. Do you?"

"Yes, mommy! He seems nice. I want to see him again, mommy." Noah exclaimed with a big smile on his face. Apparently he loves everyone that gives him chicken nuggets.

I let out a small laugh and kiss his forehead. "I think I want to see him again too, bud."

Yes, I really do. After talking to him today, I realized he could also be a nice guy. I knew there's a side of him that's not cocky. He doesn't even mention about his dirty intention on me during our talk, which I'm grateful for.

I don't know if I should protect myself and stay away from William, but staying away from him is impossible because he always have his way to make me talk to him. Maybe I should give whatever this thing is a chance. I should give it a try and see where it brings me.

And I hope with all my heart William would do the same.

-----

please VOTE, COMMENT AND FOLLOW!

Chapter 7

Jane's POV

I grab my purse and hurriedly make my way to the front door. I kiss Noah's head when I meet Noah and Mary at the living room.

"Goodnight, love. I'll see you tomorrow morning, okay? Sleep early!" I told William.

I turned to look at Mary, "I'll be going now, Mary. Take a good care of him! Bye."

"Bye, Jane. Be safe!" I heard Mary said before I closed the front door.

As you can see, I was eager to leave. It's not that I'm excited to do my job. Actually, tonight I don't have to walk all the way to the pub. No, I didn't bought a car. William is picking me up!

Have I mentioned that we exchanged numbers that time we had lunch together? Well, we did. He said he would be visiting the pub too so why not he picks me up and we could go together. I said no at first, but he insists. So that's why I'm pretty excited right now to see him.

I saw William was leaning against his car while tapping away on his phone. As I got closer, William sense my presence and look up to me. He put his phone in his back pocket and open the passenger door for me. Such a gentleman.

"Hello, Jane." William smiled.

"Hello, William. Thank you, you don't have to go all gentleman with me. I can do it myself you know." I said as I got inside his car.

William get inside his car, start the engine and drive towards the pub.

He put his hand on my thigh. "You look nice in that coat babe, but I'm sure whatever you're wearing underneath is even nicer."

Me and William started to flirt now and then but William knows his limit. This cocky side of him will always stay in him and I can't change that. It's not like I want to. I enjoy his sneaky comment sometimes. It turns me on, every time.

"Trust me, whatever I'm wearing underneath this, is not nice at all." I winked at him.

I can heard his sharp intake of breath. I guess I'm turning him on. Oops.

When we arrived at the pub, I went straight away to the back room to change while William went to the bar to have a drink.

Tonight, I'm wearing a purple lace strappy chemise. I'm excited to see William's reaction when he see me in this outfit.

I walked my way to the podium. I saw Danny on the modern jukebox trying to choose a perfect song for me to dance to.

The intro of Wicked Games by The Weeknd started playing. People has gathered around the podium and cheered for me.

"You look hot as always, Sexy J!" I heard someone from the crowd shouted at me.

I turn around once the first verse begins. I prances down the podium, my heels clicking against the stage. I waves to some guys who are hooting and hollering at me. My dark brown curls pounce up and down against my back.

Once I was at the end of the podium, I grip the pole and swing myself around it. I drop it low, shaking my ass. I bring it back up and leans my back up against the pole. Sliding down it, I kick my legs up in the air.

"We love you, Sexy J!" A man screams from the crowd.

I whips my body around the dancer's pole and with my legs out in a V-shape, I climbs up it. I wrap my legs around the pole and bends backwards.

I saw William eyes darken. He looked at me like a lion ready to pounce on its prey.

I never actually care about anyone from the crowd while I was dancing. I only dance, drink and went home. But now, William has all my attention.

William slowly make his way to my heart without him knowing. I told myself don't get attached. I'm a single mother who works in a pub as a pole dancer while William is a CEO of a huge company and probably have his breakfast on bed every morning. But it's hard not to fall for William. He has dreamy eyes, toned abs and a successful life. William always have my attention and he always keep an eye on me too.

Some of the guys from the crowd are grinning feverishly at me. I only nod and turn my attention back to William.

"Fellas," Danny's charismatic voice announces over the loudspeaker, "Put your hands together for our one and only, Sexy J! You're killin it tonight, J!"

The crowds went wild. I don't like the attention but I keep it cool.

Everybody's watching me but I was only looking at him.

-

William's POV

The music booms in the background as more people enter the pub. Men are howling and drooling over Jane on the stage. It disturbs me.

I glance at the crowd just for a second, not wanting to look away from Jane. She was absolutely mesmerizing. I always had a thing for dancers but none like this. She dances and moves around the stage with such grace. She was beautiful. I had to see more.

All attentions are on her. Everybody's watching her but she was only looking at me.

Before I know it, Jane freezes and the music ceases. The lights on stage go down and the house lights come up.

A few minutes later, the beautiful and talented Jane comes toward me, but she freezes in her steps when she saw me. She inhales deeply and then exhales. She then skips her way over to the bar.

"Hey, baby." I called for her.

"William." Jane sit at the stool beside me and turn her body so she would be facing me.

"You were amazing just now. That sexy body of yours never fail to amazed me." I told her.

Jane looks down to the floor and then looks to the side. She's probably avoiding eye contact. Her face is blushing. I can tell that she was feeling shy.

God, she's cute.

"Stop it, will you?" She shakes her head and then stand up from her stool, "I'm leaving."

I can't let her leave. Not yet. Besides, I intend to send her home tonight so she don't have to walk all the way home alone. It's dangerous for her. I don't know why the hell I cared so much about her, but she has a son at home. And if anything happens to Jane, who's gonna take care of Noah?

Great, now I care for both Jane and Noah. What the hell, William?

"Wait, where are you going?" I also stand up from my stool ready to follow her.

"I'm gonna go change, this chemise is making me uncomfortable." Jane says as she make her way to the back room.

I follow her and lean down to her ear and whisper, "Can I join? You know I'm good at undressing people. I can undress you from this sexy chemise in just a second babe."

Jane looks at me from under her eyelashes and give me her sexy smirk. That's all I need as an approval to follow her to the back room.

Jane's POV

When we get inside the back room, William sits down on the lounge suit. There is an awkward silence until William finally ask me to join him.

I step forward, walking closer towards William. I spread my legs, putting a knee on each side of William and sitting on his lap. I run my fingertips across William's cheek and down his neck. Just a couple centimeters away from William's lips, he whispers, "I think we can have more fun than that."

I look into his eyes. I don't want to fall for him again. I'm not gonna sleep with him and then being left. I don't deserve that. William is still the same cocky CEO and playboy that I know. But there's something about his look, the way he looked at me and the way he touched me. I crave it. I crave him.

"I think we can too," I growl, smirking.

William then goes for it. He presses his lips against mine and I melt into him. Our mouths open simultaneously. Tongues sliding back and forth, small moans escape from my throat.

William places his hands on my waist and moves them down to my ass and thighs. I run my fingers through William's hair as the kiss gets deeper and my moaning gets louder.

No, this is wrong.

This can't happen. Not again.

But I'm so weak when it comes to William.

"S-stop. We can't do this." I push myself from William.

"What? Why not?"

"William, just because you've known me and met my son, it doesn't mean that we can just do this whenever. Just because you're rich while I'm a single mom who is desperate for money, it doesn't mean you can use me and then leave me again. I'm not that kind of woman, you know that."

"Jane-"

I cut him off, "No William, please. I'm sorry but I think you should go." I stand up from his lap and give him way to leave through the door.

"No Jane, I'm not leaving. What do you mean we can't do this? I know for fuck sake that you want me just as bad as I want you. Don't even deny it, Jane." William said, his voice getting higher each time.

I looked at him and this time his eyes are no longer filled with lust but anger. Or maybe, sorrow?

"William, you know I have a son at home waiting for me. I can't be your fuck buddy or whatever you called it, okay? Even if I don't have a son, I still won't sleep with you. You might don't do relationship, William, but I do. I want to be with someone who really wants me in their life, not just in bed."

I looked at William one last time before I left him alone in the back room.

-

William's POV

What the... fuck?

Okay, yeah I might not do relationship and all that but was I really that bad that she doesn't even want to have sex with me again?

Was it because I left her the last time that we had sex? She should have known though, that I would leave.

I know she have a son and she's not like other women who sleep around but fuck I still want her.

I had a desire to protect her, take her places and spend as much time getting to know her and Noah as I could. The thoughts filled me with excitement, but also felt strange to me.

Usually I wanted to get rid of the woman I'm sleeping with as soon as possible. I dreaded it when they suggested movies or dinner at a fancy restaurant. They were all same and boring. But she wasn't. Jane was different. She is exciting, independent, courageous, and beautiful. Actually no, she is more than that. Exquisite, she is. And I wanted more of her. So, so much more.

I'll do anything to have her again.

Jane, just you wait.

-----

please VOTE, COMMENT AND FOLLOW!

Chapter 8

Jane's POV

I don't get enough sleep last night.

I mean how can I sleep when my mind was being occupied by the thoughts of William the whole night.

This morning I didn't have the strength to make breakfast so I laid in bed until noon. Poor Noah, he keeps whining for me to make him pancakes.

Oh baby, mommy is so sorry but mommy's not in the mood today.

At 1 pm I decided to get off the bed and take a shower. I put on some clean clothes and change Noah's as well. I'm too tired to make lunch so I wanted to take Noah to the nearest diner and have our lunch there.

After lunch, we walked our way back home. We decided to not take the bus because the bus was crowded with people today. It's almost possible for us to get a seat so we walk home.

"Mommy, can we go to the park?" Noah asked me.

"Baby, the park is on the opposite way. It's too late to turn back now, let's just go home yeah? We can watch movies instead." Honestly, I'm just not in the mood to go anywhere. I wanted to go home cuddle with Noah and maybe get some sleep after last night. Besides, the park is on the opposite way and I'm too tired to turn back.

"But mommy.... pwease?? I want to play! I want to play!" Noah looked at me with pleading eyes.

Oh god, how can I say no to this kid?

"Okay Noah, how about we go home and mommy play the leggos with you? Sounds fun right!" Actually no. I don't plan on playing with Noah today but if it could stop him from asking me to go to the park then I'll just go with it.

Noah looked away from me. He pull his right hand from me and walk away with a frown on his face.

I hate seeing him sad. Damn it, Jane! You're such a bad mother!

"Baby! Noah! Hey, wait up for mommy!" I called for him.

I tried to catch up to him. Once I'm beside him I take his hand back in mine.

"Noah! You cannot walk away from mommy like that. What if someone take you away from me?" I never meant to scold him but I was worried.

Noah only nods his head but he is still not looking at me. I can tell that he is still sad that I won't take him to the park.

"Baby... mommy is so sorry okay? Don't you wanna go home and play with mommy?" I asked him slowly.

Noah shake his head slightly, "But I wanna go to the park! I wanna play the swing!"

"Well then let's go to the park!"

No, I didn't said that. I turn around only to be met with a very handsome and casual looking William.

Oh god please... what does he want now?

"Uncle Will!!!" Noah let go of my hand and run towards William.

"Hey buddy! How is my cute little boy?"

Um... excuse me? His cute little boy?

"Uncle Will... mommy is a meany! Mommy don't want to take me to the park!"

How dare my son betrayed me, I thought playfully.

"What?? How could your mommy don't want to take you to the park? That's okay bud. I'll take you there okay? You wanna play the swing right? Let's go..."

William hold Noah's hand and they started to walk away.

So.... they're just gonna leave me here? On the sidewalk... alone.

"Are you just gonna stand there or are you going to come with us, mommy?" He asked me with a smirk. No, it wasn't Noah. It was William.

I walk faster towards them and try to get Noah back.

"I'm sorry Mr. Winston but this is my son that you're taking with you. We were just about to go home before you came. So if you'll excuse me, I'm gonna take my son back and we're going home now." I took Noah's hand and pull him with me.

"Mommy I wanna go to the park." Noah whined. "Uncle Will! Uncle Will! Help!" Noah is struggling to release his hand from my hold.

"Noah! Stop it!" I said sternly to Noah.

William come closer to us when he saw our little struggle.

"Jane... just let me take him to the park. It's not a big deal. He just wanna play. Let the kid have some fun for once." William said.

I scoffed, "What do you mean? You think he never had fun? Excuse me mister, I might be a single mother and not financially stable but that doesn't mean I'm a bad mother! I know how to take care of my child! I bought a lot of toys for him to play and I've took him to the park a few times before so don't you dare said that I'm a bad mother! And you mister, why are you even here? Are you stalking me or-"

"Woah, woah there... slow down. Catch your breathe. I never said that you're a bad mother. I'm just offering to take him to the park. You can tag along if you want okay?" William told me while rubbing my arm soothingly to calm me down.

I take a deep breathe and let out. Noah has finally released himself from me and ran towards William.

William chuckled at him.

"Okay, okay. Fine. Let's go to the park." I give up. Forget that I'm tired, I'm not even in the mood to be tired anymore.

"Yay! To the park! To the park! To the park!" Noah shout cheerfully.

The three of us walk slowly to William's car which was parked alongside the road.

The park was not so crowded when we arrived. There are only a few people here. Noah was playing on the slide while William and me sat at the nearby bench.

William looks at me and smile slightly, "You're not a bad mother, Jane. Just because you refused to take Noah to the park, it doesn't make you a bad mother."

"What?" I asked.

William only shake his head and then look back at me, "Earlier, you said a couple times that you're not a bad mother which makes me think that you thought yourself as a bad mother and earlier you just tryna convinced yourself that you're not."

I put my head down. That's actually kind of true but I just don't want to admit it.

"Jane, I'm really sorry about last night. I can't sleep cause I kept thinking about you." Well it makes the two of us then. "I was on my way to your apartment when I saw you and Noah on the sidewalk. I know you're trying to forget about last night but can we just talk about it, please? I don't want us to be like this and-"

"Like what William? Like what, huh?" I interrupt him.

William sighed. He looked at Noah who is now playing at the swing with another kid. The kid's mom is also there with them so I know Noah would be fine playing there.

"Honestly Jane, I don't know. But what I do know is that I want you. Not just in bed but also... you know..."

"No, I don't know William. Tell me, also what?" I asked him. I wanted to hear from him. I want to what he wants us to be.

"I-I don't know. I want you everywhere like... no I don't mean everywhere like anywhere but, oh god why is this so hard!" William exasperated.

He looks frustrated so I decided to take matters on my own.

"Okay, so you want me not just in bed but also... in... your life?" I guessed. Hopefully my guess is right because I'm already falling for this guy.

"I don't know. M-maybe? But life is such a big word I-I just thought that maybe I just want some company. Yeah, that's it! I want a company. You could be a friend or I don't know, just someone to talk to, I guess."

"Talk and sex?" I asked him curiously.

He looked at me shocked, "Y-yeah... I mean if you're okay with-"

"That's basically called fuck buddies you know... or friends with benefit? Yeah, something like that." I told him.

He only nods. I'm guessing that he's still waiting for my answer.

"Listen, William. You know I don't do-"

"Yes, yes I know that already. That's why I thought we should take it slow. I really want you Jane." He said in a soft voice.

"So if I said yes, you'll stop sleeping around right? You'll consider on dating and-"

William cut me off, "No! I mean... well you know I'm used to that so it might take a while to completely stop."

Wow, I definitely didn't see that coming.

"So you can sleep around with another girl while you're dating me? Oh my god William that's cheating!" I exclaimed, clearly not liking where this is heading.

"I don't mean it like that! And I don't even think I'm ready to date anyone-"

"Oh just shut up! You want me but you don't wanna date me? Whatever, William. I'm taking Noah home. You can come back to me when you're ready to be in a relationship."

I stood up from the bench and walked away to get Noah.

William was left there dumbfounded.

-----

please VOTE. COMMENT AND FOLLOW!

Chapter 9

William's POV

Shit!

I totally fucked up!

Jane is so hard to get and I have no idea what else to do to get her. My charms of being a rich and handsome CEO obviously not working on her.

I need help to get her, but who could help me with that?

Noah?

No, I'm not using her son just to get her. That sounds so wrong.

Think, William! Think! You're a god damn CEO for god's sake and you don't even know how to get a woman like Jane?

But Jane is not just any woman. She's different. She don't want me for my money and obviously not for sex either so it makes her different. Besides, she has a son. She's been struggling all this time to find money for her son. She is such a strong woman and that's why I love her.

Shit, did I just said love?

If money and sex won't make her want me then what?

Suddenly it felt like there's a light bulb above my head because I just found out one way to make her want me.

If I make her jealous, perhaps she would realize that she actually wants me too and then she would come back at me and begging for me to take her!

Genius, William! Genius!

-

Jane's POV

I'm in the back room at the pub. I was preparing myself to go on stage.

It's been a few weeks since I saw William. The last time I saw him was at the pub 3 days after we went to the park. He didn't visit the pub since then.

He probably has moved on from me. And I'm sure as hell need to move on from him too.

Damn, I sounded like we just broke up from a long time relationship or something.

After almost an hour I straddle, swing, grind and hump the pole, that's when I saw William.

But he's not alone. He's with a girl. A very pretty one.

They looked very intimate together and it makes me sick. I don't know why but I hate seeing him with another girl. I'm not supposed to care but I did.

I stop dancing because I can't do it anymore, not when William is here being flirty with another girl while stealing a few glances at me.

What is he up to?

I sit on a stool at the bar while William and the girl are sitting way too close to each other at his usual seat.

I admit, I was filled with jealousy but of course I didn't unleash it.

William would give me smug looks once in a while which was awfully sickening.

And then the worst thing happened, they kiss! That of course made the girl feel ecstatic but it made me boil with anger. Thank god it's only a short kiss but I still think I'm gonna puke.

I know that I shouldn't be feeling this way but I can't help it. I actually really did fall for him and I've seen the better side of him, the non cocky William, and now seeing him with someone else, kissing... oh, it breaks my heart!

I shouldn't have trust him. I thought that he would at least try to change and stop flirting and sleeping around with other girls but no. He's still the same William Winston that everyone know.

I don't like this William. I want the William that knows how to make casual talk with me and always found the way to make my son smiling and happy. I want that William.

I look at William and the girl, they're still flirting at each other. But I can see that William is still trying to make me look at him. No, it's more like he's trying to make sure that I'm looking at him.

If he was trying to make me jealous then he's definitely successful because I honestly can't wait to rip the girl's head off.

-

William's POV

I could feel that my plan was working. I was going to make Jane jealous. She would look at us once in a while so that means my plan was probably working. But of course she had that stupid poker face on.

Well, Stella, the girl that I'm with tonight was really annoying but I had no choice but to enjoy her presence because that's the only way to make Jane jealous. Honestly, this plan is utterly childish but I'll do anything and whatever it takes to have her. I want to make her mine.

I turn my gaze to Jane and she looked as if she was ready to go for a war but she still had this poker face on.

Damn woman, you sure did know how to control yourself eh?

-

Jane's POV

After a while of stealing glances with William, he finally make the next move.

William stand up from his seat along with the girl. He drag the girl with him to the dance floor.

Great, now they're dancing together!

Wait, no. Actually it's more like grinding on each other.

William looked like he really enjoyed himself with the girl. After this, they'll probably spend the night together.

Will he kiss her as passionate as he kissed me? Will he compliment her and tell her how great her head giving skills are just like he did to me? Is he going to enjoy and savor every moment of it with her?

Thinking about William and the girl do it on the bed together makes me hurt. Really hurt.

But I couldn't show him that I'm hurt. He couldn't know that what he's doing with that girl is affecting me. I need to look strong and act like I don't care.

I tilted my face upwards and trying my hardest not to let the tears brimming at my eyes fall down.

Oh William, why are you doing this? You're such a beast! A beast that I should forget and let go!

-

please VOTE, COMMENT AND FOLLOW!

Chapter 10

Jane's POV

I got up around 8 am with dried tears on my face.

Last night's event still burning inside my head. It's obvious that William was trying to make me jealous, probably because I rejected him. Remind me not to mess with him because he sure do know how to make someone suffered.

I'm still in bed and I turn my gaze from the ceiling to the sleeping little angel beside me. I kissed Noah's cheek and his eyes slowly opened.

"Good morning baby.vGet up, we'll have breakfast and then I'll take you out so we could get ice cream." I told him when his eyes were fully opened.

"But mommy... I wanna sleep." He replied.

"Nope! C'mon get up!" I said tapping his nose. Noah just rolled over to his other side. I sighed and went over to the bathroom.

After a few times I finally managed to made Noah left the bed. He was all dressed, sitting on the couch, watching some morning cartoon show on the TV.

I walked over to him and he looked up at me. "Baby, ready to go?"

"Yes!" He said grabbing my hand as he stood up. Noah is so excited to get ice cream so we only had a cereal bar for breakfast.

We arrived at the ice cream shop and Noah quickly made me ordered his chocolate flavored ice cream.

We were eating ice cream at one of the booth in the ice cream when Noah asked me about William.

"Mommy, when is Uncle Will going to take me to the park again?"

I sighed, "Baby, uncle Will is a busy man. He's not always going to be here if we want to go anywhere."

"But mommy... uncle Will said if I want to go anywhere then I can ask you to tell him." Noah said.

"Noah, listen to me. You must not get attached to uncle Will okay? He's not always going to be here for us. He's only my friend and he's also a very, very busy man. So let's not bother him anymore yeah?" I told Noah.

Noah only nods, "Okay mommy..."

By hearing his voice I knew that he is sad. I feel bad for him. I hate seeing my baby sad.

Damn you William for putting me in this situation!

-

Revenge

I decided to get revenge on William after what he did to me nights ago. He wants to play this game then come on, let the game begin.

I won't let William get the satisfaction of seeing me jealous while seeing him with another girl. No, I'm going to show him that I could do better. He enjoyed seeing me jealous? Well then, let's see how he's going to act when he's the one who's jealous and riled up.

It was hot in the pub tonight. The mass of dancing figures took up most of the space on the small hardwood dance floor. There are also people leaned against the walls, resting after dancing for too long.

I saw William on his usual seat, drinking one of the oddly colored drink that were always served at the bar. As he finished drinking and looking around, his eyes finally rested on me. A small smile came to his face when he looked at me. His blue eyes were wide with excitement and then he was looking around the pub again, taking it all in.

Oh, poor William, the rich CEO doesn't know what's in store for him tonight.

My hair was down loose flowing in waves over my shoulders. I was wearing a light blue top with matching tight skirt that showed off just the right amount of skin.

William continued to stare at me, looking at my ivory skin and noticing the way I was swinging my hips slightly to the music.

Suddenly, I saw a tall guy with brown hair was eyeing me. Perfect, looks like I've found my victim.

I smile at the guy when I saw him coming my way.

"Hey, you're the Sexy J right?" The guy asked me.

"That would be me." I winked at him.

The guy let out a chuckled, "I knew it, actually I saw you get down from the podium just now so yeah I'm kind of already know who you are. Anyway, I'm Paul."

"Ah yes! Nice to know you Paul." I replied.

"You too J. I have to be honest though, you look much more hotter closer." Paul smirk slightly at me.

My face flushed with a blush that was usually or recently caused by William alone. Suddenly, Paul grabbed my hand, "Let's dance." He pulled me onto the dance floor and wrapped his arms around my waist while I put my hand around his neck.

Paul looked down at me and and pulled me closer so that our hips ground together when they moved. He leaned down to my ear, "Are you enjoying yourself?"

I nodded.

He moved his mouth from my ear down to my neck, kissing along my collarbone. I can't help but let out a small moan. I can tell that the sound made Paul want to grab me and pull me somewhere private where he would be free to do whatever he wanted to me.

Suddenly, I remember William. I looked around the bar and saw that William was still on his seat while giving me a death glare.

Okay... what the hell is that for?

Oh my god! Is it working? Is he really jealous?

I love seeing him like this. But jealousy also didn't look good on him because he looked like he could kill someone with those eyes.

But I want to make him madder. I want to riled him up with anger and jealousy.

My fingers wound through Paul's hair and we danced closer. I got more confident and started to press myself against him, sliding up and down, I can heard him groaned my name into my hair.

I looked over at William. His face was cold as he returned my gaze. I only smirked in triumph.

I turned my gaze back at Paul and we kept dancing. We danced for a while and I have to be honest, I enjoyed it. Probably because it's been a while since I dance with someone.

Suddenly, Paul was being pull from me and get thrown across the dance floor. Everyone gasps.

I saw William in front of me and he gave me a death glance before he went to Paul and picked him up by the collar.

"Don't you fucking dance, touch or even look at her again! That's my girl!" William screamed while giving Paul a punch on the face.

I was shocked, "Stop! William, enough!" I screamed at him.

William let go of Paul and looked at me.

I'm honestly mad at him. What the hell is his problem?

I mouthed sorry at Paul who is still clueless and hurt.

I took one last look at William before I turned and ran towards the exit. I can feel William began to run after me. I pushed past the people standing outside the pub. I disappear around the corner at the end of the street.

I can hear William is calling my name. His voice sounds near so I ran faster. I'm already halfway down the road when suddenly someone grabbed my wrist, pulling me to face them.

"Jane! Jane, please wait!" I looked up at him.

"What the hell was that?" I screamed at him. He flinched at my tone.

"I'm sorry, I can' help it I was-"

I cut him off, "In the pub, you punched him in the face!"

"Listen, I was just-" Again, I interrupts.

"Just what huh? A-and you said that I'm yours! What the fuck? Since when, William? I was never yours!" I exclaimed.

"Damn it Jane! You have no idea how mad I was and you absolutely have no idea what you did to me back there!" He looked like a mess. A hot kind of mess. I really want to kiss him right now.

Ugh, control yourself Jane!

"What are you talking about?" My face is red from the cold and yelling.

"Because... I was jealous." He says quietly. So quite I barely heard him.

"What?" Yes, I know I was trying to make him jealous and it worked but I never thought he would acted this way and ended up admitting that he really is jealous.

"I was jealous!" He yells and slams his fist into the brick wall that runs along the street. He leans his forehead against the wall and tries to control his breathing.

"I can't help it Jane. I saw the way he look at you and the way he flirt with you. I just get angry and jealous seeing you soo close with him. I don't like him touching you like that! Hell, I don't like it if any guy ever touch you like that again!" William confessed.

I gasped.

"Fuck! Jane... what did you do to me? Please. I just need to know that you want me as much as I want you." William pleaded.

I can't believe what I'm listening to right now. This is crazy. Am I crazy?

I sighed. "William, if you really want me then show it. Prove it to me that you really want me." I told him.

And suddenly, William looked at me with his bright blue eyes. This is it. I'm giving him a chance for him to prove himself to me that he really wants me.

"I will Jane. I will, because I really do want you." He said, determined.

As the night went on, I couldn't help but think how did Danny handle the mess that happened at pub tonight. Oh, he's going to kill me.

-----

please VOTE, COMMENT AND FOLLOW!

Chapter 11

Jane's POV

It was finally Saturday. I was watching Toy Story 3 with Noah when I got a message from William. He said that he wanted to take me and Noah out at 6 pm.

I guess this is one of his way to prove that he's change and he really wants me so I agreed to go out with him. But of course it's not a date, I mean, Noah is also going with us so it doesn't count as a date right?

When I got out from the shower I put on a dark denim jeans with a mint green top. Once I was finished changing Noah to one of his cute amazing outfit, I threw my hair into a messy ponytail. It was 5:40 pm when we were finished so for the next 20 minutes I packed my purse with my phone, keys and a packet of biscuit for Noah as well as watching a bit of SpongeBob while we're waiting for William.

At exactly 6 pm, I heard a loud knock on the door. Noah was filled with excitement as he ran and opened the door. Once the door was opened, we were greeted with a smile and charming blue eyes who belonged to no other than... William.

"Uncle Will!" Noah shouted cheerfully.

"Hey, buddy. Are you ready to go?" William took Noah's hand and hold it.

"Yes Uncle Will!"

"Alright, alright." William chuckled before he looked at me, "Hello Jane. You look beautiful. Anyway, we should probably get going."

"Thank you." I nodded and grabbed Noah's hand in mine.

We walked to his car and get in. William started the engine and began to drive. We drove for about 10 minutes before the car stopped outside a big funfair.

"A funfair?" I asked.

"Yeah, I thought that Noah would love funfairs." He said.

It warms my heart knowing that he actually thought about my son, Noah.

"Mommy, mommy look! It's a funfair!" I looked at Noah and smile adoringly. He has never been to a funfair before so it makes me happy seeing him this excited.

"This is his first time going to a funfair. I'm sure he's going to love it." I said to William.

I can tell that William looked a bit shocked but he didn't show it.

"Well then... what are we waiting for. Let's go!" William looked at Noah with a big smile that showed his teeth.

I grabbed Noah's hand as we followed William to the ticket booth.

"3 wristbands, please." William asked the ticket booth man. The man smiled and passed us the wristbands which we would wear to get on the rides.

I felt like a 5 year old girl again. I honestly can't wait to try all the rides and games.

We stayed at the fair for almost 2 hours riding all the rides, playing all the games and eating a lot of candy. We were about to leave when Noah saw a big teddy that he wanted. We went up to the game, payed for it and started throwing balls at the cans. We had to play like 8 times when William finally won that bear for Noah.

The man handed the bear to William and then William passed it over to Noah.

"There you go." William said.

"Thank you Uncle Will!" Noah said while hugging the bear on his left hand and hugging William's leg on his right hand.

William chuckled playfully before he squats down the same level as Noah and hug him. My heart flutters at the sight of them hugging. William is so good and nice to Noah, I didn't know he had this side of him. William would be such a great father someday.

Poor Noah, he need a father's love and care but I couldn't give it to him. But I'll do anything to be the best parent for Noah.

Tonight is definitely amazing, Noah looked so happy which makes me happy. William even won him the stuffed bear that he wanted which made him a double times happy.

"So are you guys hungry?" William asked us once we get in the car.

"Mommy, I'm hungry..." Noah whispered to me but of course William could still heard him.

"Well... let's go grab something to eat then." William said.

"That would be nice." I smiled at William.

William started the car and drove to a nearby diner, it took only 5 minutes to get there.

I had pasta while Noah ate chicken nuggets. I told him to eat something else but he demanded to have chicken nuggets. William always being nice to the kid of course he ordered a big plate of chicken nuggets for Noah.

After we payed for the food, we quickly got in William's car. When we got to my apartment Noah hugged William and said thank you. William kissed Noah's head before he let go of him.

"Thank you so much for tonight, William. I'm sure Noah had so much fun at the funfair." I said once Noah went to the room because he was already sleepy.

"No problem. I had fun too. He's such a fun kid, I should probably take him to funfair again." William said, smiling at the thought. "And... what about you? Do you had fun?" William asked me.

I nodded slowly with a small smile, "Of course I had fun. It's been a long time since I went to a funfair. God, I missed riding all those rides you know. Especially the ferris wheel, that was my favorite!" I blushed when I realized that I probably sounded like a kid.

"You're cute when you're blushing. Anyway, I'm glad you enjoyed it. I would definitely take you out again next time, maybe without

Noah? As in a date?" William asked carefully, wanting to take it slow and afraid of my answer.

I looked down at my feet as I felt myself blushing again, "Y-yeah, why not."

William only smile adoringly at me, "I should get going, you're probably tired after riding all those rides. Goodnight, Jane."

"Okay. Goodnight, William. And thanks again for tonight, I've never seen Noah so happy before."

"Jane, from now on I would do anything to make Noah happy. So if you ever need anything like a ride to go anywhere with Noah, just give me a call and I'll be there. You can count on me." William said.

I was stunned at his words. Is this real or just an act? I can't tell but I really hope he meant every words he said.

"Thank you, William. But I don't think we'll ever need anything from you and we also don't want to bother you. You're probably busy during the day-"

"I'm serious, Jane. You and Noah are my priority now. Just please, promise me you won't hesitate to call me if you'll ever need anything okay?"

"O-okay." I nodded.

I waved one last time at William before I closed the door.

I walked quietly to my room to not wake up Noah who was sleeping soundly on the bed. He looked so cute sleeping with the stuffed bear that William won for him. I was thinking to put the bear on the corner of my room but Noah hugged the bear so tight which almost impossible for me to take it from his hold. I changed into my pjs and jumped in bed beside Noah. I kissed Noah's head and went to a deep, peaceful slumber.

-----

please VOTE, COMMENT AND FOLLOW!

Chapter 12

Jane's POV

After that night we went to the funfair, William has been texting me all day and visiting me at the pub every night. He even pick me up and drop me home, "It was dangerous for a beautiful lady like you to walk home alone at night. I will pick you up and drop you home every night from now on. I'm taking no risk and I feel better knowing that you went home safe." That's what he told me.

Tonight, I'm wearing a tight full length singlet with a high waisted short. I walked to the podium and turned sideways then started grinding my hips. If It Ain't Love by Jason Derulo started playing.

I placed my hands on the pole and spun around it. I did a split and whipped my hair. I stood up and began walking forward around the pole with my inside arm holding onto the pole. I hooked my inside leg around the front of the pole and bring my outside arm to the pole. Similar to the martini spin, I extended my outside leg but angled it downward and point my toes.

I can feel William's eyes on me the whole time I'm dancing. I steal a look at him while licking my lips. He replied with a smirk.

I stood straight up with my back to the pole and both arms holding onto the pole behind me. I extended one leg forward and point my toes. I began sliding down the pole while bending the knee of my supporting leg.

I saw William mouthed 'sexy' at me and I swear I can't control myself from blushing. No one seems to notice our flirty glances at each other and I'm glad for it.

As usual, William drove me home again tonight. I was about to walk inside my apartment when I felt someone hold my wrist, stopping me.

"Jane, can I talk to you for a minute?" William asked me.

I turned my body so I'm facing him, "Yeah sure. What is it?"

"First, you look incredibly hot tonight. That moves you made at the pub tonight made me crazy, ya know. And second, I was planning on taking you out again. This Sunday, perhaps..." He said with a smile. "With Noah of course." He added.

I blushed hearing his words. My face is probably as red as a tomato right now. Without thinking I just nodded at him, "Sure. What time? And where?"

"Great! I pick you guys at 1 pm. It's a surprise but I'm sure Noah would like it there." William said while grinning.

I nodded casually at him. "Okay then."

"Oh and just wear something casual, it might be a bit hot during that time of day." William told me.

"Wow, I'm getting more curious at where you would be taking us but yeah sure, something casual, okay." I smiled.

"Right, you should get inside now. Noah is probably waiting for you." William said while gesturing to my apartment.

"Alright, thanks for sending me home. Goodnight William." I waved at him.

"My pleasure, goodnight Jane." He waved back with a smile.

-----

short chapter, i know. this is just a filler and im trying to get this book going. anyway i still hope that you enjoy the pole dancing scene because i do!

p.s. i actually did listen to if it ain't love while writing this so yeah that's how i get the feels for the pole dancing scene

please VOTE, COMMENT AND FOLLOW!

Chapter 13

Jane's POV

It's finally Sunday and Noah was so excited to go out. We were in William's car and finally arrived at the destination.

"Oh my god baby look! We're going to the zoo!" I said to Noah as I looked up at the 'Zoo' signboard.

"Are we going to see the elephant, mommy?" Noah asked me with his eyes wide looking at the zoo's signboard with various animals illustrations on it.

"Not only elephant, Noah. There are other animals too like penguins, giraffes and even monkeys." William replied for me.

"Yay! I wanna see them! I wanna see them!" Noah said excitedly.

"I knew he was going to like it." William said while winking at me. I only smiled at him as a thank you. This guy always know how to make Noah happy. My heart warms at that thought.

Once we were inside the zoo, I make a point of getting Noah to read up on several specific animals beforehand in order to know as much about them as possible before I let him see them live.

"Okay, where do you want to go first buddy?" William asked Noah.

"Penguins!" Noah screamed.

We slightly ran towards the penguin section trying to catch up with Noah who was already halfway there, he was just too excited. This is his first time going to the zoo and seeing the animals so I won't blame him for being so hyper today. Besides, I love seeing him like this. He looks very happy.

"Mommy! Uncle Will! Look at the penguins! They are sooo cute!" My son squealed as he pressed his face against the glass in the underwater penguin viewing area.

"They're almost as cute as you baby!" I laughed while taking a picture of Noah looking at the penguins. I also may or may not secretly took a few pictures of William who is now standing beside Noah and looking at the penguins as well. The sight of the two of them together in a picture makes me smile. They looked adorable.

"Mommy... uncle Will... can we go see the giraffes pwease?" Noah asked from on top of William's shoulder.

"Sure we can buddy." William said.

After a while Noah is walking again because he said that William was too slow and he wants to reach the giraffes area faster but I took his hand before he could even run, "Noah, what did I told you about manners?" I asked him sternly, "You're not going anywhere without us, now say sorry to Uncle Will and then we walk together until we reach the giraffes area."

Noah only looked at his feet while saying, "I'm sorry, Uncle Will... can we go now mommy?"

"Hey bud, don't be sad. I'm not mad, it's fine okay everything's good. Now c'mon let's see the giraffes!" William said to Noah.

Me and my son follow William as he navigates his way through the large crowds of people.

"Mommy look! The giraffes are so tall!" Noah squeals at the sight of the large and tall animal.

"I know baby. Look at their necks, it was very long too!" I told Noah.

I was busy looking at Noah who was still mesmerized looking at the large animal for the first time that I don't even noticed William who is standing right behind me.

"I know something else that is long too, you know." William whispered to my ear.

"I-I..."

"You're blushing again. Fucking hell, Jane. Stop being cute and looked innocent, I don't think I can control myself." William whisper shout at me.

"Then don't." I said without thinking. "I-I mean y-you don't have to c-control y-"

"Shit! I swear to god Jane you're making me-" William's words was being cut by Noah's pleading voice.

"Mommy.... I'm thirsty." Noah whined.

Me and William instantly looked at Noah.

Oh my baby!

Thank you for saving me from that embarrassing situation!

You're my little hero!

"Aww my poor baby. Let's go get you something to drink, yeah?" I said while holding Noah close to me.

"Yeah, I think we've been walking for too long. Let's go find some drinks and then we'll get ice cream." William said. He is definitely not affected by the situation just now seems he looks so calm.

"Ice cream?! Yay!" Noah shouting for joy.

After getting the infamous panda shaped ice cream, Noah is now looking at the elephants while William and I took a seat on the bench right beside the elephants cage area.

We are both looking at Noah who had a big smile on his face. I am happy to see Noah who had so much fun and even I enjoyed myself so much that I almost consider to extend our trip today for a little longer.

"Thank you, William. You're making him the happiest kid in the world right now." I almost shed a tear seeing how happy Noah is.

"You don't have to thank me. I'll do anything I can to make him happy." William replied.

"I know, I'll do anything to see that smile on his face too." I said while smiling adoringly at the sight of Noah.

William chuckled, "You know what? Noah is one hell of an adorable kid. He's also very cheerful. I wonder where he got that... from the mommy perhaps?" William smirked.

"He is adorable and yeah very cheerful too." I laughed, "But I don't think he inherited it from me. I-I guess it was probably f-"

"Hey, hey let's not talk about that bastard yeah?" William told me. I chuckled at his choice of word and then nodded my head. I don't like thinking about my ex boyfriend during this happy moments too anyway.

"Jane, I have a confession to make." William stated.

I looked at William curiously, "What is it?"

"After today, I just realized that I'm actually happy. Like really happy. I feel content and I only feel that when I'm with you and Noah. Crazy, right? But it's true though. I've never felt so happy a-and free. I only feel that when I'm spending my time with the both of you. Whenever I'm with you, or Noah, all the stress from works and other stuff just gone, like poof! Gone!"

I was shocked at his words. I honestly can't believe that William just said that. It's not just me, but Noah too? I'm glad that he found happiness in Noah as well.

I told you, that kid is a freaking ball of sunshine.

William continue, "And I also realized that I smile and laugh a lot when I'm with you two. It's crazy how you and Noah could do that to me. I don't even know how but whenever I saw Noah smile or laugh it makes me smile too. And god, let's not start with you Jane. The things you did to me, I bet you don't even know that you affected me that much huh?"

Okay, forget what I said. Shocked would be an easy word.

"William, I-I don't know what to say."

"You don't have to say anything, Jane. I just want you to know how much you and Noah mean to me." William told me.

Suddenly, out of the blue William placed his strong hand on mine.

"I really, really like you, Jane. I hope you feel the same way but I'm not forcing you. You take your time, okay? I want you to be comfortable with me."

"William... I think, I think I l-like you too. Really like you." I said quietly.

William's face lit up and I can see his blue eyes are bright with happiness.

"Jane, you don't have to say that just to make me feel okay. You have to meant whatever you sai-"

I interrupts him, "I'm serious! I do like you too William."

William only smiled and tightened his hold on my hand, "Thank you. You don't know how happy I am right now."

I swear there's a firework inside my stomach right now!

"Yeah, you don't even know how happy I am too." I replied with a blush.

For the rest of the day, we walked and looked at the other animals until Noah felt sleepy.

-----

can you believe that we have reached 1K reads?!! omg thank you so much!! i love you guys!!

please VOTE, COMMENT AND FOLLOW!

Chapter 14

Jane's POV

"Alright baby, mommy's gotta go to work now. Bye, love you!" I said as I kissed Noah's head.

"Bye mommy! I love you!" Noah replied.

"I'm going to work now, Mary. I'll be back at 12!" I shouted at Mary just as I closed the door and ran down the stairs.

Tonight I have to walk to the pub. William said that he would be a little late so he told me to go first because he had a meeting.

I was wearing a strapless mid thigh black dress under my hoodie. To go with the dress were my black high heels with a diamond accents. I know, hoodie and high heels didn't go together but it's not like anyone cares. Besides, I'll change to a dress once I have arrived at the pub.

As usual, after arriving at the pub, I greeted Danny with a "Hey!" and a kiss on his cheek. Now, I am doing my routine, slowly gliding my body up and down the hard, cold pole. My strong legs hoist me up the pole as the song ironically plays in the background. Throughout the whole dance, I can't stop thinking about William. He's still not here yet.

I begin walking forward around the pole with my inside arm holding onto the pole. Using my outside leg to gain momentum, I swing and hook it around the front of the pole. As my inside leg leaves the floor, I bring my outside arm to the pole. I crossed my legs at the ankles as I slide down the pole.

Then I whip my head around to face the people watching, that is when I see William casually walk through the door. He turned his head to look at me. He smiled at first before showing me his famous smirk. I saw William went to the bar. He ordered a drink from the bartender and then his gaze is focusing on me again.

I got tired of dancing on the pole so I decided to go down to the dance floor and dance. Who knows, maybe William would want to dance with me. 'Side to Side' by Ariana Grande started to boom out of the speakers. I wiggled my hips side to side slowly. Someone's hands grabbed my waist and began rubbing against me.

I smirked to myself.

I knew he would come.

"Couldn't resist me could you, William?" I asked smirking and moved my hands up to run them through his soft blonde hair. Only they weren't there. Instead I felt short spiky hair.

"The name's Calvin, babe." The person whispered in my ear.

I whirled around and came face to face with a black hair and brown eyed man. He was tall with huge biceps. Anyone would say he was attractive, but he was not William.

"Excuse me," I said trying to step around him. He remained where he was.

"You're quit sexy, which suits your name, Sexy J huh," He said licking his lips. Alcohol was evident on his breath causing me to gag.

"C'mon baby, dance with me." He said stepping closer to me.

"Get away from me!" I snapped angrily, "Go away!"

"You're a fiesty chick aren't ya," He said grabbing my wrist, "Let's see how you are in bed."

Before I could register what he just said to me, I was being dragged by him.

"Stop! Help!" I screamed.

"Shut up!" The man growled and dragging me forward harder.

"Don't you dare touch her!" William growled at the man who was dragging me.

"Who the fuck are you? Get outa my way!" The man said.

"I'm her boyfriend. Now get your dirty hands from her!" William screamed at the man. My heart leaped at the word boyfriend.

"Woah, okay," The man let go of me, "I didn't know she was your girl. Now we're cool, right?" The man backed off, putting his hands up in defeat.

"Get out from here if you don't want to get punch on the face bastard." William growled.

The man only nodded and scurried away.

"Thank you." I said at William.

"No worries. Some of the men here are just fucking prick." William muttered, eyeing the room. "Are you, okay?" William asked, gently wrapping his arms around my body. I flinched but then relaxed under the warmth and comfort of his arms.

"I-I'm okay now," I stuttered. I tried to speak again, "H-He... He-"

"Shh, it's okay," William said. "I've got you, I'm here now okay."

"B-But he-" I started.

"I know, it's okay. That douchebag won't bother you again yeah? Don't worry, I'll always protect you Jane." He soothed interrupting me.

I cowered into William, burying my face in his neck.

"Don't worry, Jane. I'm here now. I've got you."

The two of us began walking out of the pub. People were still dancing as if nothing happened at the dance floor 15 minutes ago. Finally after what seemed like eternity, we were outside. William started making his way to the car.

Once we're in his car, William put his arm around my shoulders while I leaned my head against his shoulder. It's not a comfortable position, really, but I'll take whatever it is to be close to him.

I started to feel sleepy. William must have noticed this because he said, "Get some sleep, Jane. I'll wake you up when we arrived." I only nodded my head, too tired to speak.

I drifted off to a deep sleep thinking, William has saved me today. He might as well be my hero.

-----

please VOTE, COMMENT AND FOLLOW!

Chapter 15

Jane's POV

Tonight was a big night for William. He was about to close one of the biggest deals the company had in awhile, one he worked on for months now. And to say the least, he went all out. They are also going to have an office party tonight as a celebration. Let's just say William demanded me to come and he wouldn't take no for answer.

This morning I woke up with a big white box wrapped in a pretty little red bow, in front the front door. Once I opened the box, I was surprised to see a very beautiful navy blue dress. The custom made dress was probably more expensive than my entire apartment together. Needless to say I even looked better once the dress was on me. The blue complemented my eyes and accentuated my curves just the way it needed to.

Noah is already sleeping and I have Mary coming over to look after him. After a few minutes of waiting, a black limo showed up.

Apparently, William couldn't pick me up because he is busy with the other big CEOs so he sent a limo and a driver to come and get me.

I made a quick chat with the driver, Andy, throughout the drive to the W.W. Inc building. He was very nice and friendly for someone who seems to be in his early 50s or something.

"We have finally arrived at our destination, Miss Rosenfeld" Andy said.

"I told you to just call me Jane. Anyway thank you for the nice ride. I never imagine about getting into a limo but look at me now. Haha."

Andy only let out a small laugh before replying to my words, "Mr. Winston is never to treat any girl this way. He is willing to let you ride in his limo just to make it up to you for not being the one to pick you up. You must be a really special lady to him then."

I can't help but blushed after hearing Andy's reply. I don't know about William but I can assure that he is special to me.

Helping me out of the limo, only a minute after and I was already at the entrance of the amazing W.W. Inc building.

"Jane!" I looked up and saw William ran at the sight of me.

I had to admit he looked extremely polished tonight. William had a slick black suit on, just right for his broad shoulders and built figure. It's not hard to notice his buff muscles showing through the black suit he wore.

"You look absolutely gorgeous." William made his remark for the night with a devious smile on his face.

"Well, you look rather okay cleaned up." I gave him a smirk.

I just realized that all eyes were on William and me now. But our eyes only focused on each other.

Suddenly, an old man, or maybe a businessman, came to approach us.

"Mr. Winston." The man said.

William turned his gaze from me to the old man that interrupt us.

"Ah! Mr. Schmidt! Glad to see you here." William said with an enormous grin.

Mr. Schmidt smile and shook William's hand, "Always such a honor to be part of this eventful occasion, Mr. Winston. I see you've brought quite a beautiful young lady here tonight."

I can feel that Mr. Schmidt's word is making William a bit tense.

"This beautiful lady right here is Jane. My partner for tonight." William calmly introduced us to each other.

I smiled and nodded towards Mr. Schmidt, "Nice to know you, sir."

Mr. Schmidt playfully winked at me. I suddenly feel a bit uneasy.

"You too Miss Jane." Mr. Schmidt nodded at me before looking at William, "Well William, as much as I'd like to talk to you about our plan to collaborate, I rather get to know your beautiful lady friend-"

"Date. She's my date. Now, I believe Jane is thirsty so why not you go and have a drink first, babe?" William asked me.

My heart flutters at the nickname. I smile towards the gentlemen before saying, "Alright, nice chat but I am really in need of a drink right now so I'll leave you gentlemen to discuss about your important plan."

I hurriedly make my way to the dessert section but before I could even move, William took a hold of my wrist and whispered in my ear, "Be careful. I'll catch up to you later, I promise it won't take long."

"Don't worry. This is your night. Go and enjoy it. Don't worry about me, I'll be fine." I smiled one last time before making my way to the dessert section.

-

William's POV

I leaned against the bar with Jane ignoring the drunken antics from my employees that surrounded us. I watched as couple danced and raised their glasses together in celebration.

So many of these people would be going home or to a hotel with a drunken office hookup. The thought makes me feel disgusted. I may be a sexual deviant but at least I have Jane and I am faithful to her. I gulped down the last of my whisky, enjoying the burn down my throat as I surveyed the whole floor flooded by people dancing.

I turned to look at Jane.

"Would you like to dance, Jane?" I asked, taking her by surprise. I am all smiling and hoping that she would say yes.

Jane shook her head at me, "How convenient of you to ask. Of course I'll say yes."

I offered my hand which led to her taking it.

The song suddenly switched to a slow, soulful and a really beautiful song to dance to. Obviously Jane thought the same because the smile on her face never disappeared. Her arms naturally wrapped themselves around my neck, pulling me closer as my own hands made their way to her hips, slowly swaying to the rhythm of the beautiful piece.

"You look beautiful tonight. Really, really beautiful. Gorgeous." I whispered into her ear, my lips caressing her ear.

"Thanks, Mr. CEO" her choice of name to call me made me chuckled.

Another song came on, this time slower and more romantic, building an atmosphere along with it. Tonight is great. Dancing with Jane makes me feel alive.

I love it.

I love this.

Or maybe I just love her.

-----

please VOTE, COMMENT AND FOLLOW!

Chapter 16

William's POV

I've been waiting for this day. I finally realized that I was too in love with Jane and I was ready to take the next step with her. Every time I'm with her she always makes me happy. Every time a man is trying to get close to her I will be discontent and jealous. All these things make me realize that I may have fallen in love with Jane. I am so much in love with her.

And Noah... though he is not my biological child but his presence always makes me feel happy and relieved. My love for Noah comes naturally and I can't help but to love him like my own kid. I like to see him smile and laugh. When I see him happy it will surely make me happy too.

Jane's fortitude in raising Noah made me feel very impressed with her. No matter how big the obstacles and challenges Jane needs to face but she remains strong and always adheres to her life principle to give Noah the best and make sure their lives are organized.

But I do not want to see Jane trying so hard in raising his son anymore. I will take care of them well and provide enough for them. I will make sure their lives are happier. With all the money I have I think it's more than enough for them. I know sometimes I'm a very busy guy but I'll try my best to spend more time with Jane and Noah.
-

I was sipping my coffee when I feel like someone is watching me. I look up and see Jane is watching me with a quizzical face.

We were drinking coffee on the couch at Jane's apartment while Noah sat on the floor focusing on watching the cartoon on TV.

"What?" I asked her.

"Well, first of all it's Saturday and you suddenly came here without telling me first. Second, you somehow looks gregarious..?" she said in a tone of inquiry.

I just smile a little before shrugging, "So what if it's Saturday? I thought I am welcome to be here anytime. Besides, it's weekend and I don't have to work today."

"So you finally decided that weekend will be your days off work? No offence Mr. CEO but I thought you're an everyday working man and nothing can separate you from your jobs and ridiculously important meetings." Jane said with a smirk on her face.

I focus my view on Noah before replying, "Hate to break it to you pretty girl but not anymore. From now on, my weekends are only meant to be spent with important ones."

I stole a glance at Jane and saw her face reddened like a tomato.

God, Jane is so cute when she's blushing.

At least now she knows where she stands in my life. Jane and Noah had become very important to me recently and I can't deny the fact that they might as well be my first priority now. I am more than happy to spend my weekend with these two. I also don't mind at all if I have to spend my entire life with them.

I smile at the thought of spending my life with Jane and Noah. Waking up to a sexy woman like Jane would be a blessing. Having breakfast while play fighting with Noah sounds like home and happiness.

"Jane... actually if you don't mind I would like to ask you out tonight."

"Oh, you want to bring us out again? Where to?" Jane asked me with a surprised face.

I shake my head slowly, "No, what I mean is, uh, would you like to go to dinner with me? Just us. Like a date."

Jane has a look like she is thinking and hesitating.

"If you're worried about Noah then don't worry cause I could hire a nanny for a night to look after him-"

"No William it's not that, I was just shocked I guess." She slipped her hair behind her ears, "Of course I would go on a date with you. And about Noah I'm sure I could ask Mary to look after him tonight."

"Wait... really? You'll go on a date with me? Okay, okay... god yes! You don't know how long I've been waiting for this. Thank you for giving me the chance to prove myself to you, I'm so happy you wanted to go out with me. I promise I'll take you to the most fanciest place with great chefs and make it the best date you've ever been to."

Jane only chuckled before looking at me with a mischievous smile. She leaned closer and said, "I don't mind as long as we get to eat bagel after." She said in a sultry tone.

Fuck

Her words meant nothing special but her voice is so fucking sexy.

How did she do it?

How could words as simple as that coming out from her mouth could turn me on so bad?

Suddenly, our sexual tension was cut off when we heard a light snore. We looked at the floor and saw Noah sleeping soundly.

Noah was such a sight for sore eyes.

-----

aw this chapter means a lot to me because William finally convinced himself that he loves Jane! their date will be on the next chapter!! also it would be nice if you guys let me know if there's any concept/scene that you want me to write. request is open if you want me to dedicate a chapter for you :)

please VOTE, COMMENT AND FOLLOW!

Chapter 17

Jane's POV

I flitted through my apartment as Mary and Noah sat on the couch. With a groan, I slipped on the only heels that I owned and walked a few steps. I let out another noise of dissatisfaction and put on the black flats.

"What are you stressing about? Aren't you just going out to a dinner date with William? You should feel happy." Mary said.

"Yeah, but I can't decide what shoes to wear, and I don't know if i should wear a dress or just jeans and t-shirt. I don't know if it's going to be fancy or just a regular place. He said it was a surprise and won't even give me a single clue. He just said to wear anything nice." I shrugged with a puzzled face.

Mary gave me an odd look, "The Jane I know would not be this stressed over shoes or outfits. You would never be stressed about the simplest thing."

Mary pushed herself to stand beside me. I felt my cheeks get hot and turned my back to her.

"What's going on dear?" She asked calmly.

"Nothing, I just want to make a good impression and trying to look decent." I said quietly.

"Nuh-uh. That's not it." She teased and I frowned. "You still have an hour before he says he'll get out of work but here you are stressing. Now tell me, what's wrong?"

I sighed, "I don't know Mary. I am happy and looking forward for this date ever since he asked me that one time. But I feel like there's just something not right."

I still remember the first time he asked me on a date. But then he had to cancelled it because he got a last minute meeting. And now it has been weeks until he finally got the time for this date.

"I mean, he's a CEO for god's sake and look at me, I'm just a random girl with a lower status who dance at the pub every night. And let's not forget to mention that I'm also a single mother." I sighed.

"Yes, he is a CEO and a well known person. And yes, you are a mother to a very lovely boy and yes, you are a pole dancer because you loves to dance and you also do it for money to survive. There's not one flaw about you my dear." Mary told me with a sad smile.

I turned to look at my son who is still sitting on the couch, watching TV. And then I turned back to look at Mary.

"Jane, just because William is rich, it doesn't make him any better than you. You don't have to dress fancily just because you're going out with a CEO. Just dress up nicely and be yourself. Why change yourself for someone who wouldn't change anything for you? If he really likes you, he would still think you look beautiful even in a pajama."

All the things that Mary said to me makes me aware and feel overwhelmed. What she said also reminds me of my mom because mom always said that we are the most beautiful when we are proud to be ourselves.

"Thank you Mary. I know I should not feel inferior." I hugged her for a while.

"Okay, I go get ready now yeah? I'm just gonna wear that black dress with this black flats. Who cares what I wear? Besides, dress is appropriate for every occasions. Fancy or not, I think the dress would do the trick anyway." I said confidently while picking up my black flats and went to my room to change.

"Now that's the Jane I know." Mary said while looking at me amused and let out a small laugh.

After an hour, William arrives at my apartment to pick me up. I grab my purse and get ready to leave.

I saw Noah fell asleep on the couch. I kneel beside him and give him a kiss on the forehead. "Love you baby. I'll be home soon."

On my way to the front door I saw Mary on the kitchen and went to hug her.

"Thank you so much Mary. Thanks for making me feel okay again. You are like a mother figure to me. Thank you for supporting me in everything I do." I told her truthfully.

Mary pats me on the back, " You are a wonderful person, Jane. I want you to always remember that okay? Now go, Mr. CEO is waiting." She winked at me.

"Thanks." I chuckled. "Take care of Noah. See you later tonight, bye!" I waved to Mary one last time before I heard her, "Bye Jane. Enjoy your date!"

Once William and I arrived at our destination, my eyes went wide at the sight of the beautiful and fancy restaurant. This look like the place only for rich people.

Suddenly, insecurities wash over me and I start to feel like I am totally out of place. Unlike William who looks dashing, handsome and confident as always. Now I actually realized that I am totally out of his league. I don't belong here.

My insecurities went as fast as it came when William took my hand, hold it dearly before kissing it. He smiled at me, letting me know that everything will be alright with him by my side. I smiled back, not wanting to ruin this night for the both of us.

William opened the door for me. I giggled and walked inside the fancy restaurant.

"You look beautiful babe." He whispered in my ear from behind, putting his hands on my waist.

I blushed and looked at the ground. He just chuckled and put his hand on the small of my back.

I straightened my black dress. As I looked up he held out his arm for me like a gentleman and I take it.

"Table for two?" The man at the entrance asked while pulling out a list of paper.

"I reserved a table in the back." William spoke and the man started to go through the list.

"Mr. Winston?" The man asked looking up. "Right." William replied pulling me closer to him.

"Follow me please." The man said.

I walked after the man who led me to a table in the back but still in sight for others. William pulled my chair back and pushed it back to the table after I sat down.

"Thank you." I smiled. He was just so charming.

"You like?" William asked curiously.

"Of course, it's amazing." I said buzzing.

"Glad you like it, Jane." He smiled back.

After having our meal which consists of a very heavenly pasta carbonara, I can't help but feel satisfied. My belly feels a little too full and my face might even be a bit puffy after all the indulgent and delicious meal that we had tonight.

"Thank you." I smile gratefully as I sip the glass of wine before placing it back upon the restaurant table.

"What for?" William says while giving me his lopsided smirk.

"This, tonight, it's lovely." I said while looking at him with a genuine smile.

William reach to take my hand in his, "I should be the one to thank you for giving me the chance to take you out for a date. For giving me the chance to prove myself to you. I don't even know how I get so lucky to have this night." He says while tracing delicate circles on my hand.

"Would you two like the dessert menu?" The waiter ask approaching our table with two menus in hand.

"Oh, yes, we woul-"

"Actually, no, thank you. I think we'll have our dessert at home." I smile politely.

The waiter eyes widen a little before he nods.

"I'll go get your bills then." He smiles before turning and walking away.

"I cannot believe you just said that." William laughs covering his mouth with his hand.

"What?" I shrugged innocently trying not to laugh.

"You're so dirty babe." He laughs quietly while shaking his head.

I roll my eyes, "Like you weren't thinking the exact same thing." I smirked, "But honestly, I just want to get home early to see Noah. I miss him already."

"Are you sure it's because of Noah? Or was that just a reason for you to get us home early because you couldn't stand not touching me anytime soon?"

We both keep sending each other dirty remarks and flirty glances when suddenly I was cut off when I see a man staring at me.

"Jane? What's wrong?" William asked.

"Nothing. Everything's fine." I shrugged.

I try to ignore the man but I still see him staring at me. William noticed and turned in the direction I am looking at and he immediately gets up.

"William, don't." I said. I grab his arm and pull him back down.

The waiter returns and we pay our bill before exiting the restaurant. We get ready to leave but not before we both heard the man who has been staring at me said, "Hello there beautiful."

"Just leave me alone." I defended myself with William beside me.

"Mm, I like em feisty." The man said, smirking.

Before I could even reply, William step in front of me and look directly at the man, "Get off mate, she's mine."

The man only smirk and then looked away. William pull me with him to exit the restaurant and getting into his car.

William's hand rests upon my thigh for the most of the journey to my apartment while tracing patterns and slowly traveling higher and higher up beneath my dress.

"Nobody flirts with my girl." He said, more to himself.

"Yeah, your girl. I like that." I nodded, approving his choice of words.

I smile and kiss him on the cheek. This was a very interesting dinner date. Definitely one I'll never forget.

-----

please VOTE, COMMENT AND FOLLOW!

Chapter 18

Jane's POV

I'm sitting in the kitchen when I hear the doorbell ring and I glance at the door, wondering who would it be.

"Hmm," I say, looking at my 3 years old son, Noah.

"We should go see who that is, shouldn't we?"

"Yes mommy!!" I can't help but smile as he nods solemnly, mesmerized even more everyday by his cuteness.

"Okay, come on then." I say, scooping him out of his chair and hoisting him onto my hip as I walk towards the door.

I was completely caught off guard when I open the door to see William standing there.

"Hey, Jane. Hey, buddy!" he says, "I figured I'd stop in and see if you both wanted to get lunch or something?"

"Uncle Will!! Yay, uncle Will is here!" Noah jumped out of my hold and went to hug William's leg, "Mommy, can we go out with uncle Will, please? Please mommy..." he whined.

I put my hand on my chin and pretend to think, "Hmm... I don't know..."

Noah made a sad face to me then looked at William and tugged at his pants to get his attention. William only chuckled and bent down to pick Noah up in his arm.

"C'mon Jane, I'll take you guys to some restaurant that I just fou-"

"Nuh-uh, we are not going to any fancy place for lunch. I would only go if..."

"If..?" William asked curiously, eyebrows furrowed.

"If... we are going to McDonald's!" I said excitedly!

Noah laughed and clapped his hands, "Yay mommy! We're going to McDonald's! We're going to McDonald's!"Noah said in a sing song tone.

"Now baby, don't be happy just yet, we still don't know if uncle Will would want to go to McDonald's..." I said while stealing a glance at William.

"Uncle Will would take us to McDonald's, I just know it! Because he likes you, mommy!" Noah said enthusiastically, "Rite, uncle Will?"

"That is true, I like both of you so much that I'm willing to take you guys anywhere you want. And McDonald's? Really, Jane? You know I'll take you to the moon and back if you ask me to."

My breath caught in my throat at his words. My insides were jumping for joy, my heart was beating so fast that I could almost hear it in my ears.

"Hehehe." Noah giggled, looking at both William and me. "I told you mummy! Uncle Will likes you!" Noah said while giggling happily.

So, here we are 15 minutes later, eating cheeseburgers with coke for both William and me, and a chicken nugget Happy Meal for Noah.

I have finished my burger so now I'm sipping on my coke when William decided to clear his throat and talk to me.

"It's been awhile since I ate a burger, let alone a cheeseburger." He stated.

I forced a smile, somehow his words managed to made me feel uncomfortable. Of course he don't usually eat burgers, he's a CEO, he only eats at fancy place or maybe even got a maid that will bring breakfast to his bed everyday.

He wouldn't go to place like McDonald's and eat burgers or even try to eat fries with ice cream because that's just not him.

"Jane? Hey Jane, are you listening?" I was brought back to reality when I felt a hand on my shoulder. I looked at William and once again forced a smile.

"Sorry. Yeah, I'm fine. It's just that I'm so full and I feel sleepy now. Maybe Noah and I should head home now, eating too much can actually makes you tired, ya know." I turned to Noah and he also looks like he's about to fall asleep on his meal. I took the last piece of the chicken nugget and eat it before I stood up and hoisting Noah onto my hip.

William looked at me with a puzzled expression. "Um, wait Jane, I-"

"Thank you so much for the lunch. Don't worry about us, we can go home by bus. Bye William." I told him and quickly walk away.

"Hey Jane, wait up!" I was already five steps ahead when suddenly William came running beside me.

"Hey, could you slow down please? What was that anyway? Why are you suddenly trying to avoid me?" William asked. His face didn't look sad, but is a bit confused and puzzled by the situation.

"I'm not avoiding you." I shrugged. "I'm just tired and wanna go home. Unless you want me to pay you back for the lunch then okay I'll-"

"Oh god Jane, we're not going there again. I don't want to talk about this again. You know well enough that I don't care about who's paying what, I don't care about money-"

I cut him off, "Oh of course, of course you, the CEO of the W.W. Inc, doesn't care about money. Because you have too much money and you have no idea what to do with it so you just decided hey let's spend all this money on this pathetic woman and her son so they would think I'm nice and maybe, just maybe she would let me have her on the bed again because she's that low and pathetic!" I screamed out at William. He looked shocked and sleepy Noah is now wide awake after hearing my loud banter.

At least there's no one around us to witness it. We purposely choose to eat on the second floor which luckily have no customer eating on this floor. I really don't want to make a scene but I can't help with what I'm feeling right now.

"What...the hell? Jane? What's all this about? What's wrong? Why with the sudden change of mood? Did I do anything wrong?" William is still shocked with my words but he managed to stay as calm as he can.

I sighed, "I'm sorry, I just want to go home." I took Noah's hand and drag him out of the McDonald's along with me.

We are finally out of the McDonald's and now walking on the sidewalk, "Mommy...are you okay?" Noah asked me. His voice sounds so small and he looks like he's scared.

Aw, my baby is scared of me.

I knelt down to his level and looked into his eyes. He looks like he is about to cry. I put my arms around Noah and hug him tight.

"I'm so sorry baby. Don't be afraid of mommy, okay? Mommy's okay now. You make me feel okay. Now, let's go home yeah?" I kiss him on the forehead once and then on both of his cheeks.

"S'kay mommy. Don't be sad... I want to see you happy. But why are you mad at uncle Will?" He asked.

"I'm not mad, mommy's tired that's all. C'mon, let's go home and change into our pjs then we can watch your favorite cartoon, okay?"

Noah only nodded. As we were walking, suddenly I heard a car honk. I turned around and I'm not surprised to see him. Of course he would follow us. He just won't give up, won't he?

I saw him walked out of the car and went towards us.

"Jane."

"What else did you want, William?" I looked at him with an annoyed expression while Noah is still looking clueless and innocent beside me.

"I want you to explain what the actual hell happened back there? Why are you mad at me?" William asked, clearly trying to stay calm even though I can feel like he is boiling inside with my sudden attitude.

I sighed and rub my temple gently trying to find the best answer to give to him.

"Look William, I'm sorry for being mad. I just, ugh, I don't know I just don't feel-"

"Hey hey... it's okay, it's alright now. That's okay if you don't wanna talk about it right now." William said softly. "Let's take you and Noah home first and then you guys could rest. We could talk it all through after that. Okay? Now, c'mon."

William pick up Noah in his arms and then slowly and gently hold my hand and guide me into his car. The whole ride to my apartment was full of silence and it almost suffocate me so I rub my temples, again, to calm myself.

-----

omg guys thank you so much for 100+ votes on this book!! i'm soooo happy i think i'm gonna cry! I LOVE YOU ALL!!

anyway taylor's new album 'reputation' has been released today so please buy them on itunes (or any other platform) and have a TS' REP listening party!! ;)

please VOTE, COMMENT AND FOLLOW!

Chapter 19

Jane's POV

I put down the coffee that I just made on the coffee table and took a seat on the couch besides William.

"I'm sorry that I bombarded you with my angry outburst earlier. I don't know what happened to me. I guess... I was just... I'm just..." I trailed off at the end of my sentence.

When I stopped talking, he finished my sentence for me. "Don't trust me. You didn't trust me, that's it, isn't it?"

"William, it's not that I don't trust you. I'm just i-insecure, I guess. You're a public figure, you're rich and god knows what else and then there's me, a nobody." I scowled in disapproval. "I'm sorry William, I can't help it but my insecurity always get the best of me, especially when you're around. Somehow, I always thought that you were only doing this out of pity." I said while looking down at the steaming cup of coffee on the table.

"What do you mean I did this out of pity?" William asked, his brows furrowed.

"You have pity on me! That's why you were trying to be nice to me because you feel bad for sleeping with me and then you figured that I'm a poor single mother so that's why William, that's why you were being so nice to me and Noah. Maybe you feel guilty or something, I don't know." I took a deep breath and still won't meet his eyes. He must be glaring at me this whole time I was talking.

"So, you're saying that everything I did before was just an act? You think that all of that was just an act, Jane? You really saying that it was all fake, are you freaking serious with me? God." William pulled his hair out and he looked frustrated to say the least. Then, he took a sip on the coffee that I made for him before focusing back on me.

"Listen to me, and I mean it Jane. I want you to listen to me clearly. It was never fake and it was not because I pity you. Truth is, I actually adore you even more knowing that you are strong enough to grow Noah on your own despite all these struggles you're having. And if it would make you feel better, I'm sure your dad would be so proud of you. I'm sure he's not that heartless to think of you and your son as a burden to him. I'm sure he would love you both just as much as I do." William finished his sentence while holding my hand in his.

He clearly didn't think before he speak because he do realize that he just said that he loves me, right?

"W-William, I don't think you heard yourself clearly, you literally just said that-"

"That I love you? Well no shit, I do love you and Noah. There's no point of hiding it anymore, I bet you think I was faking it again just to make you feel better huh? Hate to break it to you Jane but it's the truth." William said and let go of my hand slowly and then all at once. He looked sad and tired. Probably tired of my annoying attitude. How can he still look handsome as always even when he's sad? But despite all that, I could see the sincerity in his eyes.

I didn't think twice before I lunged myself at him. I hugged him tightly but I think he was still shocked with my sudden action because I can feel his body tensed and his hand stayed still. After a minute past, he still won't hug me back. I slowly released my hold from him, my face was red out of embarrassment.

William looked directly at me but still haven't said anything yet. I guess I shouldn't have hugged him but I can't help myself, I'm also much in love with him! When he sincerely confessed that he loves me and Noah, I didn't think twice before throwing myself at him.

"I-I'm sorry, William. I didn't mean t-to." I said in a small voice, embarrassed by my sudden attack on him.

"Jane. Why did you hugged me?" William asked.

"I'm sorry, I don't know... when you said that you love me I can't help it...I-I'm" I don't know how to say it. I don't how he would react if I said that I love him too.

"Jane, spill it. We're doing this right now, no more secrets or whatsoever. Tell me." William demanded.

I looked at William and stare into his eyes. One look at him and I can already see my future with him. I can see we sit together on the bench while watching Noah playing around in the playground. I can see myself waking up every morning next to William and then having Noah to jump on our bed to wake us up on Christmas morning. I can also see us as a family, playing around at the beach and then William would help Noah to build his sandcastle while I lay down under the umbrella with another baby girl or boy. This is the moment I realized that I really love William and I have fallen so deep for him.

"I love you," That's it, I have said it out loud. Maybe I was thinking way too forward about my future with William. I'm trying so hard to not let my tears fall down.

"Are you sure, Jane? You don't have to-"

"Damn it, William! I love you okay? I really do." I said it again and now tears are actually pouring down my face.

William smile genuinely and pulled me into his lap. "I knew it. It was a good thing because I love you too." I looked up at him and smile while he wipe away the tears on my face.

"Damn, we're not even together but the I love yous have already been said. We're going to fast, don't you think?" I chuckled.

William looked down at me with his brows furrowed, "What do you mean we're not together? Of course we are."

"Um, actually we're not really together. I mean, I'm not officially your girlfriend and you know..." I said while playing with the hem of my shirt.

"Well then, it would only make sense if I ask you this," He said and took my chin to make me look at him, "Jane Rosenfeld, will you be my girlfriend?"

I smile from ear to ear when suddenly it turns into a smirk, "Actually, I don't know..." I said while putting a finger on my chin and pretending to think.

"Jane..." William groaned.

"Okay, okay I'm just kidding. Of course it's a yes!" I said with a wide grin on my face.

William looked back at me, smiling, and put his hand on the back of my neck then pulled me forward to kiss him, "Thank you, Jane" He kiss me again slightly.

"William, you know there's a lot more commitment if you being with me, have you ever thought about it? About Noah? Once you choose to be with me, you would automatically become his father figure. He would look up to you and-"

"Yes, Jane. Of course I've figured it all out. I've thought about this before. To be honest, I really wouldn't mind spending the rest of my life with you and Noah." He tucks the stray of hair behind my ear, tilt my chin up and slowly kissing me.

I can't believe that this ridiculously handsome and rich CEO is my boyfriend. To be even more ridiculous, we even said the I love yous to each other. It happened so fast but It feels like the right time.

Everything was perfectly fine when we finally stop kissing and William stroke my hair gently. I suddenly realized that there's still a lot that I don't know about this man. Who's his family? Where do he live? What's going to happen next? Most importantly, how would Noah react to this? Would he be okay with William being his father figure?

All these thoughts keep passing in my head and I snuggled closer into William's neck as we end up cuddling on the couch. My last thought before I fell asleep was that William's cup of coffee on the table is probably cold by now and he only drank it once, damn it!

-----

please VOTE, COMMENT AND FOLLOW!

Chapter 20

Jane's POV

Today I woke up with a smile seeing Noah was still sleeping beside me and my smile grew wider once I realized that William and I are dating. I haven't told Noah yet but I did tried dropping hints sometimes by casually saying 'Uncle Will is such a great guy', 'We'll be seeing and spending more time with Uncle Will from now on', 'Would you like it if Uncle Will become your dad?'

So far Noah only gave me positive responses and I'm thankful for it. Even without asking I already knew that Noah loves William just as much as I love him. Noah always seems to be very happy whenever William is around and it warms my heart that William is more than happy to be with Noah too.

I rushed to get my coat in the closet and quickly kissed Noah on the forehead and cheek and said goodbye to Mary. William was looking around furiously before he saw me and gave me a kiss. We both get into the car and drove off to the pub.

"William, are you okay?" I asked.

William looked straight ahead on the road before looking at me and smile, "Yeah, I'm fine. What about you? And how's Noah?" he asked and put his hand on my thigh while his other hand on the steering wheel.

"We're good. Noah missed you though. He keep asking me when will his favorite Uncle Will come to play with him again," I said and remembering all those times Noah asked me about William, "But don't worry, I told him that you're a pretty busy guy and can't always be around to play with him. I'm sure he gets it now."

I heard William sighed so I look at him and hold his hand that was resting on my thigh, "What's wrong?" I asked with a concerning tone.

"I missed Noah too, so much. I hate not being able to spend more time with him and you. I'm really sorry Jane. We recently closed a deal with one of the big companies so I'll be busy for a while now."

"Oh my god, really? Congratulations baby! And don't worry about us, I totally understand. But please don't drown yourself in work too much, I don't want you to stress yourself out." I said while squeezing his hand.

"I just wish I could spend more time with the both of you especially now that we are officially together, ya know. I promise after I'm done dealing with this new project then I'll take the three of us somewhere far and less crowded so no one can interrupt us."

"So you mean like a vacation?" I asked.

"Yes, absolutely." William said with a smile.

It was really nice of him for wanting to spend more time with me and Noah but I don't want us to always be on his way and be the reason of him getting distracted from his work.

Sometimes I wonder if I even made the right choice by being with him. He's a successful CEO and pretty much busy all the time. Working and meeting new people is what he's been doing all these years and he's proud of it so I won't let myself separate him from doing what he loves.

"That sounds nice but I'm sure we could think about the vacation another time, besides it's not really necessary to be going for a holiday sooner. And William, let's not forget that I also have a job to attend to. It might not be the most successful job or something that I could be proud of but it's more than important to me because that's how I survive. I need money for rent, bills, and you know the rest." By the time I ended talking, the car came to a halt and I looked through the window and saw that we have finally arrived at the pub.

I was taking off my seatbelt when I heard William replied, "Actually, there is another thing that I want to talk to you but now is probably not the right time and place for it so we'll talk later ok?"

I looked at William for awhile before nodded, "Are you coming with me? Or do you have somewhere else to go?" I asked him.

"Baby, I would love to stay and see you on stage again but unfortunately not tonight. I got some files to go through and I need to sign them by tonight, the documents have to be delivered first thing tomorrow morning so yeah I gotta finish them."

I know I'm not supposed to be mad or annoyed, I promised not to interfere him with his works but I still can't help the frown on my face and the sad feeling in my heart.

"Oh no, baby are you mad? I really wanna stay but you kno-"

"I'm fine William. That's ok, go finish your job while I'll be here to finish my job. But you'll pick me up after right? Unless if you can't then I totally understand. I could just walk like I usually did, it's not that far from my apartment anyway." I said while giving him a smile and open up the door to get out from the car but William stopped me by grabbing my arm.

"Hey, I'm sorry yeah? And I thought I made it clear to you that I'll be the one to drop you off and pick you up before and after work? Wait for me, I'll be here at 11 tops. There's now way I'll let you walk alone Jane." William told me before letting go of my arm.

I chuckled at his words. "Alright then Mr. CEO, I'll see you soon!"

I was about to close the passenger door before I heard William screamed, "I love you Jane!"

I looked at William one last time and said, "I love you too, Mr. CEO"

-

I have just finished dancing and now making my way to the drink bar for an old fashioned cocktail. I was enjoying my drink peacefully when suddenly I saw Danny came to me with a smirk plastered all over his face.

"Hello Jane. How're you doin? By the look of it I'm sure you're in a pretty much good condition right now huh. Saw it myself that you finally get yourself a man, a rich one may I say." Danny said, still with a smirk on his face.

"Hey Danny. It's been good I guess. Don't get wrong perception about me now, you know how I am." I told him.

"So it's true then, you're really with that rich guy? William right?" Danny asked amusingly while cracking his knuckles.

"Well, you could say it like that. But all this thing is so new to me and I don't want to rush anything. I'm just glad William could accept me and Noah. You know how much Noah means to me so of course anyone that can get along with him then I'll give them a chance." I smile remembering all those times Noah and William spent together. "It took one meal of chicken nuggets for Noah to fall for William." Both me and Danny laughed, we both knows Noah is a really big fan of chicken nuggets.

"Oh god, I missed Noah. You should bring him here again sometimes, during the daytime of course." Danny said.

I nodded my head with a smile. "Yeah, I'll see if I could find some time to bring him here. I'm sure he missed you too Danny."

Danny return the smile. "That's great. But seriously Jane, I'm glad you found William. If he is really honest in this relationship then it's good. I love seeing you happy, you deserves it Jane. With William in the picture now, you and Noah can start a new life, a much better one. William can give you that."

"No, it's the other way actually, he founds me. But just because we're dating it doesn't mean I could use him and his money. I can work for a better life on my own. I'm an independent woman and I need no help from anyone." I said while feeling a little bit irritated.

I heard Danny chuckled, "That's not what I mean, I'm not talking about money. What I'm saying is that you can start a new better life with having William on your side. He could be the missing piece in your heart, he could be the guy that would finally patch up all the broken pieces of your heart. And he could be the best father for Noah. He could be the father that Noah has always needed, he will love Noah and shower him with happiness." Danny put a hand on my shoulder and looked straight into my eyes. "Noah can finally have a father that he had always wanted, it'll make him happy. William can make him happy."

There is no doubt that Danny was right. William is the answer to our missing pieces, he would be the lover that I've longed and be the best father for my little baby.

I sighed but nodded at his words anyway. "You're right. But I still won't risk anything. I don't want to get hurt again Danny. I've been living and raising my child on my own for years. I'm used to it by now. Then William came, if he really wanted to stay in our life for good, then maybe... just maybe, I'll let him stay in our life."

"Don't worry, I never found a guy, especially as rich and good looking as William, to actually fall in love with someon- I mean, ya know, someone like you. A single mother and all that. If he's willing to do this then he's probably head over heels for you." He added understandingly.

"Thanks Danny, I need that." I said idly.

"Or maybe because he found you really good in bed." Danny said with a smirk and then laughed when he saw my face.

I know he was only joking but I fake shocked anyway and hit his arm playfully. "Danny!" I gasped and laughed along with him.

"I was joking okay. But for real, I hope he makes you and Noah happy. If he ever do anything to hurt you or Noah just tell me because you know I'll beat his ass, who cares if he's a CEO or what. I'll still kick his ass for you." Danny remarked while winking at me.

I laughed again at his words. "Thanks Danny but I really hope he wouldn't turn out like that. Thanks for helping and taking care of me. You're the best brother I never had and I'm so grateful to have someone like you in my life." I said genuinely.

"You know you can rely on me anytime Jane. If you're really my sister I would be so proud of you. I'm so proud you turned into this strong and wonderful woman. I'll always be here for you Jane." Danny said. He put a hand around my shoulder for a side hug.

I said nothing, and he met my gaze once more for an assurance that I am okay.

"Thank you, Danny." His words almost bring me to tears only because I was suddenly being reminded of my dad. I wonder if he would be proud of me too.

I miss you dad.

Wherever you are, I hope you're fine and happy.

I love you dad.

-----

the ending was a little bit sad don't you think? :(

anywayyyy what do you think william wants to talk about with jane? do you guys have any idea? hmm i hope it's not a bad thing because i'm so tired of them fighting, why can't they just get along for once lol

please VOTE, COMMENT AND FOLLOW!

Chapter 21

ATTENTION! PLEASE ALERT THAT I HAVE CHANGED THE TITLE OF THIS BOOK FROM 'HIS WANTS' TO 'BEAUTIFUL DISASTER' :)

make me happy by clicking the 'star' button on the top! <3

enjoy reading! ;)

Jane's POV

The talk with Danny tonight really brought up something in me. And I recognized it as guilt. It has been years and I have been over the feelings long ago but it's back now. I was feeling guilty for leaving my dad alone. I was young and dumb at the time and I was scared so that's why I chose a stupid decision by running away from home. If only I talk to my dad first, I'm sure I could handle a little lecture from my dad but that sounds way better than running away and leave my dad alone. I'm so selfish. I didn't think about my dad first.

How is he now?

Who's taking care of him?

Is he okay?

Did he eat?

I should have never left him alone, he needs me just as much as I need him. The thoughts of going back home and search for him has crossed my mind a few times now. But I'm scared to go back to my old house.

What if he doesn't want to see me anymore?

What if he is mad at me for running away?

What if he is no longer want me as his daughter?

"Jane? Baby, you're alright?" I heard William asked me. I saw his head poked inside on my bedroom door. Noah was already asleep beside me on the bed.

William kept his promise to pick me up at the pub and sent me home. I have changed into my pjs while William made some coffee.

"Hey, come in." I said urging him inside. William looked at me from the door with his eyebrows furrowed.

"Are you sure? Is that okay?" William asked. This is the first time he's going to be inside my room and it was nice of him to ask for my consent first. He do knows that I take my personal space seriously and he respect that.

"Sure it's fine. Come here babe." I smiled at him while patting the edge of the bed for him to seat.

William returned the smile and came inside with two mugs of coffee in his hands. "Here's one for you with extra sweetener... and one for me. Black, just like how I like it." William said while handing me the mug of coffee on his right hand. I took it slowly because the mug felt hot on my skin.

"Thanks William." I said. I blew the coffee slowly to cool it off a little before taking a sip.

"Anything for you baby. So he has been sleeping since we arrived?" William asked while his right hand brushed off Noah's hair that covered his forehead.

"Yeah, Mary told me all he did tonight was coloring and eat some bread with jam." I said and put my coffee on the bedside table.

William stared at Noah for awhile before copying me and put his coffee on the bedside table. He took both of my hands and hold it.

"Jane, you know I love you right?" William asked me.

"Yes William and I love you too. Are you okay? Is there anything you wanted to tell me?" I asked him carefully, curious as to what he is going to say.

"Yeah, I kind of want to talk about something but I don't know if this is the right time though." William said while slightly rubbing the back of my hand with his thumb.

"That's okay. We could talk tomorrow instead." I said while smiling trying to lighten up his mood because he doesn't look so happy right now and I don't like it. I want to see him smile but he still looks gorgeous anyway.

William suddenly let go of my hand, "I want to but I can't, not tomorrow either, I can't tomorrow. I'm sorry Jane, I'll be busy the whole day tomorrow. It will be the last meeting of the new project and then I'll be available as always." He said with downcast eyes and a guilty face.

I smiled softly at him. "That's fine, you know I can wait." William smiled back at me. He took my right hand and kiss it.

"Besides, I also have something to tell you... something to talk about. But it can wait after you are done with this new project you're having." I told William sheepishly.

"Is it important? Did someone bother you? You can just tell me now Jane-"

I cut him off, "Nothing, everything's fine. Don't worry okay?" I caressed his cheek with my right hand while my other hand hold his hand.

"Are you sure it can wait? If it's important just tell me sooner. Are you having any problems right now? Or do you need money?" William asked.

"Stop it William!" I whisper shout. "Everything is fine. And no, it is not about money. You know that I'm capable of finding my own money right." I said while slowly letting go of his hand and making a gap between me and him.

William frowned. "Baby, I'm so sorry. I didn't mean it like that. I was just worried, ya know. But if you don't want to talk about it right now then fine we'll wait for the right time yeah?"

I slowly nodded while looking down at my hands on my lap. William lift my head up and kiss me slowly.

"I gotta go. Need to make sure the documents have been signed and delivered first thing tomorrow morning."

"Okay, goodnight William."

William kissed me again before saying, "Goodnight. I love you baby"

William reached towards Noah and kiss him on his head while whispering a 'sweet dream big guy'.

I watch as William walk to the door and about to close it before his head peak inside, "I'll make sure the door is locked before I leave. Gotta make sure my two favorite person are safe. Love you Jane." he said while winking at me and left.

The door was closed and I sighed, "I love you too"

I looked at the bedside table and saw two mugs of coffee that William made earlier. One for me and one for him. I miss him already. I wish we were staying together so he don't have to leave or I don't have to. It would be nice but I don't think William is ready for us moving in together. He probably never even thought about that. I sighed again.

-

The next morning I woke up with two messages from William, he wished me a 'good morning' and an 'I love you'. I replied the same to him and also a 'have a good day at work!'.

3 hours later me and Noah was watching TV while eating some biscuits when I got another text from William. He told me how much he miss me and Noah. I told him that we both miss him too.

Another text from him came in and he said that he will be finishing early today and will come to my crappy apartment later tonight, well he didn't said crappy but the lack of furniture and the dull decor definitely made it look crappy. Regardless, this crappy apartment is what I call home.

Hours later after watching a few reruns of Spongebob Squarepants with Noah, I walked into the kitchen to make some mac and cheese for dinner. I'm surprised that I'm still alive after not eating for hours today. At least Noah ate some bread and jam that I made for him. I'm so freaking hungry I can swallow a whole huge pizza into my mouth right now. I didn't realized how fast the time has passed by but somehow it's already 8 pm.

I took out the frozen mac and cheese from the fridge and carry it to the oven. I put a pan of water on to boil. I sit on a chair while waiting for the water to boil.

"Ugh," I moaned. "I can't wait until you're inside me, feeling me up." I said, looking at the macaroni. Then, I get up to check on the water. It's boiling. Finally, I can't wait to have the macaroni all hot and cheesy in my mouth. Mmm.

I picked up the mac and cheese and took off the lid. Then, I poured all the contents into the boiling water. My hunger makes me all hot and bothered, I don't even know that was possible.

Once it's all done, I poured the mac and cheese into three empty bowls. Yes, three, another one for William just in case if he haven't eat anything yet. Since I was deadly starving, I take one bowl of the mac and cheese and stick my fork in it. I stir it around. As I stir it around, it makes a delicious squishing sound. A moan escape my lips, just get inside me already!

I pile some of the macaroni on my fork and bring it close to my mouth. I lick the shaft of the fork up and down. I can't take it anymore, I'm so damn hungry, so I shove it into my mouth. The warmness of the mac and cheese is the first thing I feel.

I slide my tongue around the fork and the macaroni, tasting its cheesy goodness. I swallow the macaroni and its warmness slides down my throat easily.

Mmm, delicious! So cheesy and warm!

Damn, I'm not sure if I even hungry or maybe just horny.

After I was done eating my mac and cheese, I brought another bowl of it to the couch where Noah is playing with his superhero action figures.

"Hey Noah bear, I made some mac and cheese for you." I said.

"Mommy! Yay mac and cheese!" Noah said happily and sit on the floor to eat.

I was helping to feed Noah his mac and cheese when my phone rang. I picked up the call after the third ring, "Hello?"

"Hey it's me. Open the door quick, I'm here."

"William, oh okay hang on." I said and hang up the call. I quickly ran to the front door. I opened the door to revealed William wearing a pair of black dress pants and a white button down, the top two buttons undone. His navy blue tie hangs loose.

"Hi babe" William greeted me.

"Hey, come in." I told him.

William kissed me briefly on the lips and walked past me to go inside. I closed the door and walked to sit at the couch while William was sitting on the floor besides Noah.

"Hey buddy, what are you eating there?" William asked Noah while ruffling the little boy's hair.

"Uncle Will! Mommy made me mac and cheese. You want some?" Noah asked with his mouth full.

"Mmm mac and cheese, yum! Uncle Will is hungry."

I laughed. "Come on William, I made some for you too. It's in the kitchen."

"Alright, I'll be back Noah. Then we can play or watch movie together yeah?"

"Yes Uncle Will!"

I walked into the kitchen with William followed behind. I put a bowl of mac and cheese on the table for William. "Here's for you. I just thought you haven't eat yet so I made some for you too."

William sat on the chair and started to devour the mac and cheese. Just like me earlier.

"Thanks baby. I haven't eat anything since lunch."

"Yeah sure"

I took a glass from the cabinet and poured a plain water for William.

"Sorry, we're out of orange juice at the moment. I hope the water is okay with you." I said shyly. I don't really have much groceries, snacks or drinks in my fridge. It's pathetic, really.

"No, that's cool. Water is fine. I've been drinking coffee all day so right now it's probably best for me to have some plain water." William told me.

"Okay, so how's work?" I asked.

"Good, I tried to finish the meeting with the new dealer by today so I don't have to be in the office for the next few days."

I looked at William curiously, "And why is that? Are you going anywhere?"

"Now that, is what we are going to talk about tonight." William replied.

Oh darn!

-

I have put Noah to sleep and now I was sitting on the couch with William. The TV was on to show some cooking channel but the sound was being muted.

"Is he asleep?" William asked.

"Yes, so now you can tell me about what has been bothering you these past few days." I said.

William stared at TV for a moment before speaking up, "First of all, I hope you won't get mad about what I was about to say."

"That's not helping William. It depends on the situation and what are you going to say." I told him.

"I want you... to... stop working at the club." There. William finally said it.

I was shocked, of course, "What?" I shrieked.

William shifted slightly on the couch and looked at me, "Listen, I know you don't want me for my money or anything. I also know you are a responsible woman. But, since we're together now, I just thought that maybe, you know… I would pay for your expenses and all that so you don't have to work anymore."

I looked at William and I really wanted to scold at him for asking me to quit my job. So what, he wants me to just sit still at home and look pretty?

"William, you don-"

William cuts me off, "Please Jane, it's not just about the money." his voice sounds irritated. "You're my girlfriend now, and tell me Jane, which man in the world is okay with their girlfriend pole dancing, half naked for everyone to watch? Definitely not me and obviously no man is okay with that too." he exclaimed infuriatingly.

Wow, so there goes the real reason of him wanting me to quit my job then. I should have thought about it. Of course he was jealous, duh.

"Oh William, I don't know what to say…."

"Just tell me you will quit that would be fantastic Jane." he said sarcastically.

"Really William? I'm sorry okay. Fine I'll quit. But Danny wou-"

"Woah there, wait a second, Danny who?" William asked. His face scream anger. Or jealousy?

"Danny, the club owner? Remember? Relax Will, he's a nice guy. Danny is the one who helped me when I first moved here. He's the one who gave me the job and he is also close with Noah. Noah likes him too." I told him.

It didn't help. Nope. William seems more furious now. I guess telling him that Danny is close with Noah is only adding to his anger. He's jealous, I can see it. I slowly took William's hand and hold it.

"William, baby, Danny means nothing to me. He's only a friend, more like a brother. And Noah is still a kid. Well, he loves everyone that gives him chicken nugget, you know."

"So, I have no reason to be jealous of this Danny guy then?" William asked while raising his eyebrows.

"Nope, no reason to be jealous at all. In fact, you have to be glad because Danny was really kind to me and he has helped me with a lot of things. He even helped me to find this cheap apartment to stay." I said smiling at the thoughts of my first time seeing Danny.

I first met him at a bus stop. I was only carrying my medium size bag with nowhere to go and pregnant. Danny saw me from far at a burger stall and he came to me, offering to help my carry the bag since I was pregnant. He seemed like a nice guy at the time so I told him honestly that I don't really have a place to go. Danny was curious at first and I don't really want to tell him all about me so I just told him I would be fine alone.

Concern of my safety, Danny asked me to go to the nearest diner and he payed for my meal. When I sensed that he has no bad intention, that's when I started opening up to him. I told him what happened to me, about my ex-boyfriend, Adam, and about how I run away from home, leaving my dad alone.

Danny might seems like a bad guy when you first saw him, but trust me, he is far from that. He determined to help me and I was more than grateful to have him at that moment.

"Right, as long as he didn't try to pull any move towards my girl then I'm good. Because if he ever try to do anything to you, or even just think or have a dirty thoughts on you, I swear he better be prepared to have my fist collided with his face." William said while mimicking a punching moves and punch his fist into the thin air.

I laughed at his playfulness, but I know deep down that whatever he said, I should definitely take it seriously.

"Yeah okay master," I winked at him. "I'll quit tomorrow. Can you drive me to the club though?"

"No worries, I'll drive you there babe." William replied.

"Okay. So, is there anything you want to tell me? That I should change my name and maybe move to an Island far from here and far from all the male generation so you won't be jealous?"

William chuckled, "I mean, if you're willing to then I'm def- ow!"

Yep. I punched his arm.

"You better be serious Will"

"Alright, alright. I was joking."

I sighed, "Fine. But really, is there anything else? You told me earlier that you won't be going to your office for a few days. Why is that?"

"Oh yeah... about that" William rubbed his hand on the back of his neck and looked away from me.

"What is it William?" I asked him again.

"I was thinking if you, well, you know since we're together now..."

"Yes, and?"

"Jane, will you move in with me?" William asked.

I'm not entirely sure what happened to me but I can actually feel, hear my inner self screaming with joy.

-----

hE DROPS THE QUESTION! MANNN DON'T YOU THINK IT'S ABOUT TIME FOR THEM TO MOVE IN TOGETHER?!

please make me smile by clicking the 'star' button on the top!! also leave a comment if you found any grammar mistakes, you should have known by now that I haven't proofread all these chapters.

please VOTE, COMMENT AND FOLLOW!

Chapter 22

EARLY UPDATE!! thank you for all your votes and comments! also thank you for adding this story into your reading lists! every little things you do only makes want to write more so here's another chapter for my amazing readers, i love you all!! :) <3

22 is my favorite number woo!!

btw please read author's note at the end!!

enjoy reading!! ;)

Jane's POV

Today is going to be exciting and tiring. I'll be moving in with William today. William have helped to sent Noah at Mary's house for today. The past few days got me exhausted and I still wonder why because, honestly, I don't really have much things to be packed. Only my clothes, toiletries, Noah's clothes, toys, a few DVDs that I bought and some other stuff.

Oh have I mentioned where exactly I will be moving?

Have a guess.

I'll be moving to William's $7 million luxury penthouse!

I clearly haven't realized that my boyfriend is rich as hell.

I took a last glance around my tiny, cramped apartment which was now crowded with cardboard boxes. I sensed William approaching me from behind and wrapped his arms around my waist, pressing his smooth lips to my neck.

"Got everything packed?" he mumbled.

"Y-yeah, I think s-so." I said, trying to keep concentrated. Even after a month of being with William, he still had this affect on me.

"Good." William whispered directly to my ear. "Finally, today is the day babe."

"Y-yeah Will." I replied shakily. Today is the day that I will be moving into William's luxury penthouse. I was a little nervous but mostly excitement filled my body.

William pulled away from me. "Excited?" he asked amusingly.

I turned to face him. His face was lit up with excitement as he looked at me smiling.

"Oh my god yes! Imagine all the memories we are going to make living together! And I'm sure Noah would be really happy too. Oh William I can't wait!" I exclaimed excitedly.

"I'm glad you're excited because so do I. Besides, no offense, but this place is tiny. Noah can have more place to run and play at the penthouse later. And bigger kitchen, not that I would ask you to cook because you know I can just hire a maid for that." William chuckled.

"This place is indeed tiny." I laughed. "Noah is really excited to see his new home. He practically whined and promised to help me with the boxes today, as long as he could go to the penthouse sooner."

"Oh that adorable kid." William said with a grin.

Laughing, I turned back around.

"I'm gonna have a one last check." I told William, beginning to walk towards my bedroom.

"Should I ask those men to start loading the boxes into the truck?" William asked, his head tilted to the side slightly.

"Yeah sure." I replied, shrugging.

After a final check of my bedroom, toilet, kitchen and the living room, I was finally satisfied. A man was just walked back in through the door when I reached the living room, and was picking up another box. William helped to carry some of the boxes to the front door to let the other man pick them up.

"Okay, I guess I got everything." I smiled, clapping my hands. My old apartment was finally empty and now looked a bit bigger.

"Bye my old apartment. You are the first home that me and Noah ever had. Even though you're tiny but you always keep me and Noah safe and warm. I'm going to miss you, my ex-apartment." I said dramatically, walking around each room and area in the apartment with William tailing behind me.

"You are so cute babe." William laughed at me, kissing my forehead.

"And you're hot." I replied.

"Damn baby, not here " William chuckled. We both laughed.

"Let's go home." William grinned at me, grabbing my small hand in his large one and kissing it. I wrapped my arms around him and nuzzled my face into his chest.

"I love you Will." I murmured.

"I love you too Jane." William said, a smile in his voice, and hugging me back.

After a few moments, I pulled away and we both walked back down to his car.

After a 20 minutes car trip, we have arrived at William's penthouse. It was big. So big. I managed to asked William why did he even live in such a huge penthouse alone and he said this penthouse was actually a present from his parents. Okay so yeah I kind of forgot that his whole family is ridiculously rich. William used to stay in a studio apartment near his office building. But since I was moving in with him so he figured we stay at the penthouse which is much more comfortable and convenient for both me and Noah.

All my stuff and boxes is already placed in his penthouse. I started unpacking things and wanted to put them on their place but I don't really know where should I put them. More like, I don't even know where is my bedroom.

Since I have moved in his place, does that mean I still sleep in the same room as Noah or-

"Baby, what are you doing?" I heard William asked me.

"Oh hey, I just um I don't really know where to put my stuff. I don't even know which one is my room." I laughed dryly.

"Right, I forgot to show you. Here this way." William lead me into the end of the hallway and opened the door to reveal a huge, clean, neat and nice bedroom with an adjoining bathroom.

"You like? So this was my bedroom." William said while pulling me inside the room with him.

I startled for a second. "Wait, this is your room? It's beautiful, really, but I was asking of where my room is though."

William's beautiful laugh echoed in his large bedroom.

What?

Did I said something funny?

Why did he laugh?

"Baby, this is your room." And oh, that's when I realized. Of course I'll be sleeping with William, in the same room as him, in the same bed as him. Stupid Jane, why I haven't thought of that before.

"Oh, oh." I am still a bit stunned.

William chuckled, "This is our room baby girl." he whispered huskily into my ear.

"Oh my god. Oh my god. This is your room, I mean o-our room! Oh my god William!" I shrieked.

William laughed, "God Jane, you're so adorable. Well, yes this is our room now. Why? Don't you want to sleep on the same bed with me kitten?" he asked with a smirk.

I blushed. How is he so calm at this. Ugh, I hate that sexy smirk, why do he have to torture me like this?

"I'm just g--gonna go and take out my things and p-put them here. I'll be r-right back." I hate it when I stuttered. I must look like a fool in front of this sex god who is wearing only a white muscle tee, showing his perfect sculptured abs.

"Sure, but don't take too long babe. I can't wait to have you in the bedroom so we could do some fun things together." he whispered sexily into my ear before letting out a chuckle and leave me alone in the bedroom. He even managed to slap my butt before going out of the room.

I was shocked and embarrassed. I turned to looked at him walking out of the room, "Hey, my butt!" I shrieked.

"Sorry, can't help it. You got a pretty ass babe!" I heard William replied from the hallway.

My face was red like a tomato. I can't believe I'm going to be living with that sex god from now on.

Oh god please help me.

An hour later I finished putting away my things with a little help from William. We were now eating an egg and chicken sandwich in the kitchen.

"Honestly," William started, "I'm really glad that we live together now, because that means that I can see your beautiful face and hear Noah's joyful voice first thing in the morning. I can wake up everyday and know that I don't have anything to worry because you're here with me."

I looked at him with a soft smile. "Aw Will..."

"When you and Noah are here with me, I feel complete and all my worries are gone." William said. "I'm going to love you both so much and give you the happiness that both of you deserves."

I can almost feel an imaginary tear of happiness rolling down my face. He was being so sweet but I don't feel like crying so I just keep smiling.

"I love you too William. Thank you for willing to accept me and Noah in your life. Thanks for making me believe in love again. You make me and Noah very happy." I replied while smiling brightly.

"I love you more baby." William said, kissing me.

Sweet moments like this makes me happy but also feeling guilty. I don't deserve this happiness and I sure don't deserve William in my life. Meanwhile, my dad was back there at home, all alone.

"William?"

"Yes babe?"

I play with the sandwich on my plate, "I have something to tell you. It's about my dad."

At the mention of my dad, William stopped eating and turned to look at me. "Oh, okay. What about your dad? Did he found you? Did he contacted you?" William asked.

I shake my head. "No, no. I was just thinking though. I kind of miss my dad. I really miss him, Will."

"I feel bad for leaving him all alone. I wonder how he is right now a-and how did he cope with me running away, leaving him? Did he eat? Is he sick? Is he okay? I'm worried about him. I think I... I regret for what I did. I shouldn't have left him, Will. I shouldn't have run away." I sighed, tears brimmed in my eyes.

William wrapped his arm around me. "Jane baby, don't cry. I know how you feel. I know you regretted your decision but that was in the past. Don't think about some silly mistake that you did in the past. What matter is now, right now. It's good that you still cared about your dad. I think it will be better if you go and see him." he said.

"I can't go see him! Not that I don't want to, god I miss him, I really want to see him Will. B-but what if he doesn't want to see me? What if he hates me, Will? What if he hates me?" I said, looking hopeless and despondent.

"A father can never hate his child. He might be hurt, but he won't hate you Jane. I'm sure he miss you too. Perhaps, he has been looking for you all this time. I'm sure he was worried about you." William said in a soothing voice as he rubs my back.

"Thanks William, I don't know what would I do without you. I do want to see him but I'll think about it first yeah? Maybe later." I said and kiss his lips.

"Because right now, I still have a few boxes to unpack!" I exclaimed.

We went upstairs and I wanted to unpack and put away Noah's stuff in his room. Yes, Noah get his own room, which is fairly huge I might say. I can't wait to decorate the room with Noah. He must be really excited to have his own bed and room.

So yeah, that was the plan at first but this cheeky, sexy man, which is no other than William of course, wanted to cuddle. He said that I've been unpacking all day and asked me to have a little rest. He also promised to help me unpack later and also decorate Noah's room.

I sighed and fell for his charm. This guy.

We went upstairs and started to cuddle on his bed, or should I say our bed?

"I'm so glad that we are finally living under the same roof now," William kissed me and rubbed my leg at the same time. "I love you so fucking much. I can't even explain it." William said. "If only I could show it to you..."

"Show me." I whispered in his ear.

"What?" he asked me huskily.

"I s-said, show me." I repeated.

William immediately started kissing my neck roughly as he continued to rub my thigh.

"Mmm Will." I moaned.

He stopped what he was doing and he pulled off my shirt. "Baby, you're so perfect." he said as he started to pull off my bra. Then, he pulled off my black jeans, leaving me in just my underwear.

I got up and pulled off William's shirt while he was still sitting on the bed. I straddled him and started to grind my hips back and forth.

"Jane." William groaned.

He picked me back up and laid me back down on the bed. I managed to steal a glance at the digital clock on the bedside table. It was already late night. William slowly kissed my lower stomach area.

I let out a moan at the feeling he gave me. Suddenly my eyes averted back to the digital clock and that was when I realized something.

"Oh shit." I cursed.

William stopped whatever he was doing and looked up to me. "You okay baby?" he asked.

I sighed and slowly looked into William's still lustful eyes. "Will, we forgot to pick up Noah at Mary's place."

"Oh shit." he cursed.

OH NO! they were caught up in the moment and forgot about little noah :(my poor baby :(((

ATTENTION!! from now on, i won't be putting any warning on any chapter that contains mature theme! so please beware if you don't like to read stuff like that, you can just skip to the pg scene. don't say i didn't say i didn't warn you! tbh, i sucks at those mature scene so if i ever write any it would probably be mild mature, i don't know yet but sure i'll try to improve myself only for all my mature readers out there ;)

you guys are the best, ILY!! :) <3

please VOTE, COMMENT AND FOLLOW!

Chapter 23

Jane's POV

The pub is not so crowded today. During the day, the pub is much more comfortable and have less people. Only a few construction workers, elders, and some middle aged men and women who worked at the nearby building would come here to have a drink or a quick brunch during the daytime. A few kids were also seemed to be enjoying their one scoop of ice cream and fries.

Danny really did take a good care of his pub. Now, you might be imagining Danny's pub to be like those club with black decorated walls, have an expensive lounge and a sparkling disco ball hanging on top.

Wrong.

Danny's pub was decorated with a classic vintage beige grey wooden wall with old yellow antique lamps hanging. He also had that bright and colorful lighting on every corner but that was only for the nighttime use. During the daytime, the pub was much more casual, almost looked like one of those typical coffee and donuts cafe or a pizza diner. A modern but classic juxebox was also situated near the corner.

So yeah, this pub is not one of those expensive, 5 star rated, high class club. It is much more old fashion than you think.

"Enjoying the drink?" Danny asked me.

"Yeah, looks like Noah was also enjoying his chicken nuggets." I replied, chuckling.

I looked at Noah who was busy eating—devouring his one medium plate of chicken nuggets. I sat besides William with Noah in front of me and Danny sat in front of William. We were here today to tell Danny that I'm going to quit. I have told Danny earlier, he was concerned about me at first but then I told him the reasons and he was relieved.

"I really hope this won't be your last time to be here. Just because you quit Jane, it doesn't mean you can't come around anymore. You're always welcome to be here. Especially this little nugget guy over here." Danny said while ruffling Noah's hair.

"Of course we will come here again. I will never forget you Dan." I said and turned to look at William. He was drinking his coffee when he glanced at me.

William cleared his throat and looked at Danny. "Uh yes. Sure, we'll stop by here again some other time."

I looked at William and smiled. He was trying to control himself from jealousy. I am glad that he was doing good.

Here's the thing though, earlier at home before we left for the pub, I pleaded him to at least went inside the pub and have a drink. I want him to try talking with Danny and perhaps become friends with him. But of course William didn't want that. He refused to went inside and only wanted to stay in the car, waiting for me while I went inside and tell Danny that I want to quit my job. That sounds rude, especially when William is the reason that I quit this job.

William was just jealous of Danny because 1) Danny knew me first, 2) Danny knew me better, 3) Danny has helped me a lot instead of him, 4) William was jealous of how close and friendly I could be with Danny, which is ridiculous because it's only a brother-sister relationship and nothing more.

William is just really hard to pleased sometimes.

Luckily, after having a 13 minutes make out session on the couch which then was being interrupted by a loud shrieked from Noah, William finally agreed to meet Danny as well.

My hand went to squeezed William's hand as if to say "I'm here with you." and "You're doing good".

We stayed on the pub a little later than we planned but I totally don't mind because right now everything seems perfect to me. William was finally engrossed in his conversation with Danny, talking about his new project deal and sometime talked a bit about sports, which I clearly know nothing about. Meanwhile, I was busy watching Noah who is still eating his chicken nuggets and have some tomato sauce on the corner of his lip. I laughed at the scene.

Later, we said goodbye to Danny and left the pub on William's car.

"So... you and Danny huh? Are you guys like a bff now?" I teased William.

"There's nothing Jane. We were just talking." William replied casually. I can see his ears turned red, William was embarrassed because he was the one who didn't like Danny in the first place. But look at them now, chitchatting about those man stuff and all.

"Whatever you say babe." I chuckled, amused by his red face.

"Mommy! Uncle Will! When can we decorate my room?" Noah asked from the back seat. "My room was empty, mommy you promised to decorate my room soon!"

Noah's room only has a single sized bed in it with only a few of his old toys were placed on the corner. The walls in his room were covered in the color blue but empty with no decorations which made the room looked dull and doesn't seem like a little child's bedroom.

"Oh honey, I'm sorry. We'll go shopping for your room later okay?" I told Noah.

Noah huffed. "You said we can go yesterday! And then today you said we will go later! You always lied to me mommy." Noah whined.

"Alright, alright no more whining. Why go later when we can go now?" William said.

"Go now?" Noah asked bewildered, "Yay! Let's go now! Let's go now!" he chanted happily in the back seat.

I laughed.b"Okay then, now it is."

William drove us to the Ikea. Noah squealed in excitement as he saw the infamous blue building of the Ikea.

"Mommy, mommy look! That's Ikea! Ikea!" Noah exclaimed.

William and me looked at each other, we both laughed. "Hmm... looks like someone seems very eager and excited." I said.

After we parked, we walked inside the Ikea. As we entered the building, the cold temperature of the air conditioner instantly hit us. Our eyes roamed around, we even spotted a stuffed animals section from here.

Noah jumped excitedly, "Mommy, Uncle Will.... look! Look! I can't wait to go there."

We laughed and walked forwards with Noah between William and me, holding both our hands.

As we were walking, I can find lots of children's rooms ideas to choose from.

After the fifth round, we finally have more than enough things to buy for Noah's room. We even bought the kid's play mini kitchen for Noah's adorable new playroom. Oh yes, I forgot to mention that William also has another room specialize for the kids playroom. I thought it would be such a waste but William said we will be needing the playroom when we have more kids in the future. Can you tell how red my face was at the time? As red as a tomato!

I also managed to buy two plush of the Ikea stuffed vegetables. Because for real though, who doesn't need an incredibly soft, plush carrot and broccoli?

I know we're in Ikea to shop for Noah but I just can't help but plead and beg William to let me buy the pretty Ikea ornate frame. I really loved this fancy schmancy frame. I could imagine it in my bedroom or somewhere in the living room with a wonderful cursive quote inside of it.

Some of the furniture that we bought for Noah are the white and blue wardrobe, a small bookshelf for Noah's drawing and coloring books, toys storage combination with boxes, a blue swivel armchair with a matching blue rug, a small round table with its stool and a cute, white table lamp. We also bought a few stuffed animal and some stars and moon stickers to decorate Noah's bedroom wall.

Days later, all the furniture that we bought has arrived. Thankfully William came home early from work again, we spent the whole day to clean and decorate Noah's room and the kids playroom.

Lastly, we were putting things away in the playroom. The playroom was filled with a toy storage, a small round table with two chairs, a play tunnel with a matching colorful children's tent, an easel with some colorful chalks for Noah because William knows how much Noah loves to color and draw, lots of cute soft toy, a 45 piece train set with rail, a few gloves and finger puppets because I think they're very cute, a stacking game which also goes with a chess and a monopoly, and a huge, wide and soft purple rug.

William really did spoil Noah. He didn't admit it at first but then he insist and told me that was only because he wanted Noah—his kids, to have easier lives. He did not, however, want to spoil them. I don't blame him though because I also want Noah to have the things in life that I didn't have as a kid. I want to make him happy and I wanted to be the best mother for Noah.

After everything was set and done, Noah can't stop smiling. His smile only gets even wider, if that's even possible.

"Are you happy bud?" William asked Noah.

"Yes yes yes! My room is very pretty, I have so many toys and I also have an easel so I could paint and draw like a real painter!" Noah exclaimed.

"Well baby, I'm glad you're happy. Mommy and Uncle Will really love seeing your cute little smile." I cooed while pinching Noah's cheek.

Noah jumped happily. Then, he ran towards William and me, and hug us tightly. "Thank you! You two are the best! I love you mommy, I love you daddy." Noah said while still hugging the both of us.

I heard William gasped. He glanced at me and slightly raise his eyebrows. I smiled at William and nodded my head.

William gave me a knowing look and a warm smile. He patted Noah's head gently. "Mommy and daddy loves you too buddy." he said.

My heart warms at the sight and I feel like my heart is going to explode out of happiness. I hug my two favorite boys closer to me and I finally feel safe and happy to have them in my embrace.

-----

did someoNE SAY DADDY?! ;D

cuteness overload!!my heart is going to explode!!i need my ice cream float!!and you guys have to VOTE!! ;)

please VOTE, COMMENT AND FOLLOW!

Chapter 24

Embrace yourself for this chapter!! we're going to have a very long ride!!

enjoy reading! ;)

Jane's POV

I paced back and forth in front of the closet while holding two dresses on my hand and another few dresses were being hanged for me to choose from.

I looked at the emerald green, wrap front lace dress on my right hand and then turned to looked at my left hand which I was holding a red satin dress trimmed with a few maroon sequins on the chest area.

As you can see, I was having another battle with myself on choosing which dress to wear. Usually, I would just ask for help from Mary or ask for opinions from Noah. But sadly, Mary is not here. Meanwhile, Noah was busy playing, and whenever I asked him, he would only reply with, "All the dresses are pretty mommy!".

William has told me earlier that they would be having a little company party, actually it is more of a press conference, at the W.W Inc. tower building tonight. I asked him what is the press conference for and his replied was, "Nothing much, I only just decided to do a little press conference a few days ago. It was a last minute decision, really.".

He also told me that every employees of the W.W Inc. will be there, some of his business partners which are CEOs from other large companies were invited as well, and a few journalist would be there too. And the scariest part is, his parents will also be attending the press conference tonight.

So now you know why I was panicking around.

I looked at the various choice of dresses that William has bought for me when we went shopping last weekend. We also bought many new clothes for Noah. I looked at all those sparkling, beautiful dresses and finally decided to wear the red satin dress.

William will be home anytime soon so we could attend the event together. I still have like an hour before the clock strikes to 6 o'clock. Without wasting anymore time, I grabbed my towel and rush to the attached bathroom for a shower. I took a really quick shower and abruptly did my make up.

While putting on a mascara, I walked over to Noah's room. I opened the door to reveal Noah was doodling on his bed.

"Hey baby." I said.

Noah looked up from his drawing and looked at me. "Hi mommy."

"Noah, you need to change. We have to attend an event at daddy's workplace, remember?" I told Noah while struggling to do my mascara. Giving up, I sighed and put the mascara away, decided to do it properly later in the bathroom.

I walked towards Noah's wardrobe and pulled out a new clothes for him.

"Here, can you change into this on your own? Mommy's need to go change too." I told Noah while giving him a proper and neat clothes for him to wear for the event.

"Okay mommy. I can change on my own. I am a big boy!" Noah exclaimed.

I kissed his forehead. "Good boy. I'll be back to check on you okay." I said while walking back towards my bedroom.

I finished my make up by applying a red lipstick on my lips and continue putting on my mascara. I get off my robe and put on the red satin dress. I looked into the mirror and frowned. Something's not right. Then I took out the red heels from inside the closet and put it on. I turned to looked into the mirror again, and this time I am smiling, satisfied with the outcome. I reached for my black purse and put my phone, keys, lipsticks and money in the purse. I checked myself out one last time on the mirror when suddenly I heard sound coming from the front door. I smiled, William arrived just right on time.

I walked through the hallway and reached the living room. I saw William just walked in. He looks gorgeous in his black suit and, surprisingly, a matching red tie.

I saw William checked me out from head to toe. "Hey babe. You look beautiful, absolutely stunning." he said, eyes still raking over me.

I blushed at his words. "Thank you. You look dashing too. And, oh my, your tie matched my dress." I chuckled.

William laughed at my remark. "Where's Noah?"

"He's still in his room. I have already asked him to change. Should we check on him?" I asked.

"Yeah sure." he replied.

As we were about to move, Noah ran towards us, already changed into his mini version of suit just like his dad.

"Mommy! Daddy! Look, I am a CEO just like daddy!" Noah exclaimed while showing off his outfit.

"Aw my little boy." I cooed.

"Aha! Now that's my big guy. You are just like daddy now aren't you?" William said while picking up Noah in his arms and kiss him on the forehead.

"When I grow up, I want to be just like you, daddy!" Noah said.

William smiled. "Sure buddy. You can be anything you want, I will still love you no matter what."

I looked at the clock and gasped. The event will start at 8 pm, as what William has told me earlier. As much as I love to see them being affectionate like this, but we have to get going soon or we're going to be late. As for William, it wouldn't be good for his reputation if he is late to his own event. Especially, since he was the CEO.

"Alright you two, that's it. We have to get going or we're going to be late." I said, hurrying them.

William put Noah down and help to straighten his suit. "Okay, let's go."

I took Noah's hand and we all walked outside and get into William's Audi.

During the ride to the W.W Inc. tower building, I can't help but fidgeting and squirming on the seat out of nervous.

"Hey, are you okay?" William asked me in concerned.

"Yeah sure." I said way too fast and way too confident to be true.

William frowned, he put his hand on my thigh while the other hand on the steering wheel. "Tell me the truth, Jane." he demanded.

I sighed. "I'm sorry, Will. I don't know, I guess I was just scared? Nervous? Ugh, I mean how can I not? We're seeing your parents Will!" I exasperated.

"W-what if they don't like us? What if they hate me? And Noah? What if-" I was cut off by William trying to calm me down.

"Hey, listen to me. Slow down, Noah's going to hear you. And don't worry babe. They're not going to hate you or Noah. I've told them about you two so... no big deal right?" said William.

"But William what if they-"

William cut me off again, "Shh. Stop thinking about the what ifs. I'm sure they're going to love you. My parents are easy people, Jane. They're not materialistic like some other rich people."

I sighed and nodded at his words. "Okay, but promise you'll be there when I meet your parents? You won't leave me alone right?" I asked him.

William chuckled. "Of course I won't leave you. I won't leave your side, I promise. I'll always be beside you and Noah, babe."

"I'm sorry Will. I sounded like a clingy girlfriend, aren't I?" I whined.

William squeezed my thigh with his hand. "Hey you're not clingy. But honestly I would still be okay if you're clingy. It just proves that you really love me and can never get enough of me." he smirked.

"You wish." I scoffed but laugh anyway.

Later, we finally arrived at the W.W Inc. tower building. This would be my second time being here. We stopped at the 3rd floor where the event was held.

As we entered the huge event hall, I was surprised to see so many people drinking, laughing, talking to each other. They all looked strikingly handsome and beautiful wearing elegant suits and expensive dresses. I can't even tell which are the employees and which are the VIPs. They all looked very nice.

Meanwhile, I'm still just a plain Jane, wearing my simple red dress. The only jewelry that I'm wearing is a simple yet beautiful, romantic diamond necklace that William has bought for me from Tiffany & Co.

My hold on William's arm tightened as we walked with Noah in between, following us.

"Are your parents here yet?" I whispered to William while my eyes raked around the wide and busy hall. I am aware that some of the people stopped talking and looked at us. I also spotted a few girls which I assumed the employees, were ogling over William.

"They're already here but I haven't seen them yet. Come on, let's get to our table first." William ushered me along with him.

Once at the table, I saw a woman probably in her 50s, dressed in a brown dress with pearls and gold sequins trimmed over the waistline and the sleeves. She was smiling brightly and came towards us. She looked like one of those very important people, and also could be very rich based on the dress she is wearing.

"Oh there he is! My one and only son!" The woman exclaimed. No wonder her face seemed familiar, she is William's mother.

"Good to see you too mom." William greeted her with a smile.

Oh god, I can't believe this. We're meeting the parents already? I think I'm in need of a drink first.

"William, look at you. My son is still handsome as ever!" His mom exclaimed with a wide grin on her face.

William blushed at his mother's excitement over seeing him. "Mom, please." he said. "Where's dad?"

Suddenly, an old man in a very expensive suit came beside William's mother.

"Hello son." The man, William's father, greeted him.

"Hello dad," William replied. "I'm glad you could make it. I know you're not really into this type of event since you've retired. So I'm really glad you could be here tonight, especially since we have an important announcement to make."

I didn't know there would be an important announcement. I thought this press conference was held only to gathered the business partners and nothing that important, as William had said before.

"Oh yes the announcement! We won't missed it for the world!" William's mother exclaimed while smirking slightly and looking at me.

"Right," William quickly nodded before looking at me and Noah. "So mom, dad. I would like you to meet my girlfriend, Jane." he said with a hand resting on my lower back.

Remember Jane, first impression is very important. I took a deep breath and smiled. I hold out my hand to William's mother. "Hello, it's nice to finally meet you Mrs. Winston."

Sadly, she refused my handshake. Luckily, she grin widely and pull me into a hug.

"Oh hello darling. I can't believe we finally get to see you. William has been so possessive over you and won't let us meet you until today. And please, just call me Carol." Carol told me.

She hold my cheek and looked at her husband. "Look hun, isn't she lovely?" Carol asked her husband with an adoring tone.

"Indeed. Hello Jane, you can call me Wade." he held out his hand to shake and I accept it.

"Thank you, you both are very kind." I replied with a smile, trying not to look like I am trying to hard to please them.

"Alright," William said. "Let's not forget this little guy over here." he picked up Noah and hold him in his arms.

"Mom, dad, meet Noah." Said William while showing off Noah who looks a little shy at the attention he gets.

Carol gasped and went forward to caress Noah's cheek gently. "Oh dear, look at you. You are so adorable. Such an adorable kid!" she gushed.

Wade was also smiling and ruffles Noah's hair. "Hello Noah. Nice to see you kid. Do you know who we are?" he asked.

William looked at Noah and said, "Noah, these are your grandma and grandpa."

Noah's eyes went wide. "They are your parents, daddy?" Noah asked.

"Yes buddy." William replied.

"My grandma and grandpa?" Noah asked again.

William chuckled. "Yes big guy."

Noah squirmed to get out of William's hold and went to hug Carol.

"Grandma!" Noah screamed happily.

Carol looked down to Noah and ruffles his hair. "Hello sweetie. Oh, you are so cute, aren't you?" she cooed. We all smiled and laughed. I'm very grateful that William's parents could accept Noah and me. Noah also looked very happy to finally have a wonderful grandparents that love him dearly.

After that, we were all seated at the same round table and enjoy our meal while occasionally talking with each other. In the meantime, William will also bring me to meet other important people, his business partners, and he would introduce me to them. I even managed to have a short conversation with some of the other CEOs wives. It was nice to finally meet some new people.

"Shit, what is he doing here?" I heard William cursed under his breath. I looked at the person he was looking at and found a familiar looking old man, wearing a navy blue suit. The man was slightly shorter than William but he still had a strong built body as far as I can see through the suit he was wearing. That's when I finally realized who that man was. He is Mr. Schmidt. We met at an office party also held by William months ago.

"What's wrong? Isn't that Mr.Schmidt? I thought you guys are business partner." I told William. Curiosity clouding over me.

"Was business partner." he said. "I knew from the first Sullivan Schmidt was having some difficulty with his company. But I thought it won't affect my company so I made a partnership with him. Later, my company's profit decreased and I found out without his knowing that his company almost got bankruptcy because he lied to so many shareholders and have so many unsettled debt. That's when I cut off my partnership with him."

I gasped, shocked at what William was telling me. I couldn't believe Mr. Schmidt would lie to anybody.

"But that's not the only thing that is bad about him." William scoffed.

I gasped again, "There's more?" I asked curiously.

William nodded briefly, "I want you to stay away from that old man. He has once been accused of sexual assault. I don't want him to try touching, talking or even looking at you with his pervert eyes. He'll be dead if he ever try to do anything to you."

I can't believe this. How can an old man like Mr. Schmidt could be so bad to the point of being accused of a sexual assault? How can someone be so bad and evil to even lie, manipulate people and also making sexual harassment towards someone. That's just so bad. Despite Mr. Schmidt being an old man, it still doesn't stop him from doing bad things that could affect other people's life, future and career.

"That is honestly bad." I agreed with William. "But I'm glad you have cut off any kinds of partnership with him. You shouldn't get involved with someone like him." I said.

"Exactly. So that's why I was wondering why the hell that man was here. As far as I'm concerned, he was not invited." William told me.

I looked back to Mr. Schmidt and saw him walking towards us. "Stay still because your enemy is walking this way." I whispered to William.

For a moment, I thought I saw panic in William's eyes. "W-what? Oh shit." William turned around to face Mr. Schmidt. I was frozen, still standing besides William. Luckily Noah was not with us and he is currently talking and listening to the made up jokes by his grandparents. At least I know he would be safe there with Carol and Wade.

"Hello William. Ah, I was looking for you. What a nice event you have tonight. The food is good too." Mr. Schmidt said.

William only nodded. "Thank you Mr. Schmidt, although I was a little surprised to see you here tonight. But anyway I'm glad you're enjoying the food." William said, not amused at all.

"Oh come on, I thought we were on the first name basis. We used to be partners, right?" Sullivan chuckled.

"Sullivan, I believe that was before. We have form no more alliance now." William told Sullivan intently.

"So that was it? You cut off our partnership, our alliance, and now I was not even invited to one of your company events? That is plainly cruel you know." Sullivan said, chuckling.

Then, his eyes averted to me. He checked me out with his lustful eyes. I squirmed uncomfortably beside William. I don't like having his eyes all over me.

William cleared his throat and I saw he gave Sullivan a death glare. "Mr. Schmidt, I would appreciate it if you could stop ogling over my girlfriend and keep your eyes somewhere else." William said, surprisingly calmly.

"And why should I do that?" Sullivan scoffed. "You have a very pretty lady, a sight for my sore eyes. Besides, I'm only looking at her body and giving her the attention that you couldn't give." Sullivan said, smirking.

I can feel heat radiated off of William. I slowly entwined our hands and gently graze the back of his hand with my thumb.

"Mr. Schmidt, please watch over your mouth. I don't like having people like you around my alliances. And definitely not around my family." William told him, this time his voice raised a little causing a few people to stare at us.

Sullivan stand closer to William and he still have that stupid smirk on his face when he said, "Why? Do you feel challenged by me?" Sullivan leaned even closer to William and whispered, but I can still hear what he said next, "You afraid that this old man could make your girl scream even much louder than you did? What? You don't have much stamina only after the first round?"

I looked at William. "He's only trying to get under your skin. Don't let him get to you Will." I said to him.

That was it, I can already see it coming. William pushed Sullivan harshly on the shoulder. "Stay away from me and my girlfriend! You better watch out your mouth you old man!" he shouted.

"William." I hissed when I found almost everyone in the hall has their attention on us.

Even after William's little outburst, Sullivan doesn't look like he is stopping anytime soon. He is still wearing that stupid smirk on his face. This time, he laughed shortly and went to me. He stared at my breasts before looking back directly into my eyes. He holds that mysterious glint in his eyes and it makes me scared at what this man is capable of.

"Don't worry honey, if you come to me I can guarantee you that I could satisfy you on the bed more than William the weak can." Sullivan said to me and then let out a maniacal laughter.

I guess that was the last straw because not even a second later my eyes witness a very angry William throwing a punch at Sullivan.

"What a prick, I already gave you a warning haven't I? How dare you said things like that in front of me!?" William said to Sullivan who is now has a bloody nose. He deserves it though. Surprisingly, no one even ask Sullivan if he was okay. I guess everyone knows better than to interfere.

"Guards!" William shouted. A few securities and guards came to us. "Mr. Winston." One of the guards called him.

William pointed to Sullivan. "I don't want to see this man ever again. I want him out of my building!" he told the guards. Two of the guards hold Sullivan and pulled him out of the building.

"Throwing me out of the building? Really? That's not a nice way to treat your guest William! How dare you humiliate me like this!" Sullivan screamed angrily.

"You are not even invited to my event in the first place Sullivan. So that doesn't make you my guest. Get the hell out from here and don't ever come back!" William shouted back.

"YOU WILL PAY FOR THIS YOU BASTARD!" That was the last thing we heard from Sullivan before the guards pulled him out from the event hall.

"You're a bastard, bastard." William said under his breath.

"Hey, you okay?" I asked William while soothingly caress his cheek.

"Much better when that prick is gone now." he replied.

I'm grateful that the crowds finally went back to normal. They all back to having fun with each other. I'm glad what happened just now doesn't affect the press conference that we're having tonight.

I took William's hand that he used to punch Sullivan. I slowly kiss each of his knuckles. "Does your hand hurt?" I asked.

"Not really." he replied. "Listen, I'm so sorry that happened. Tonight was supposed to be a good night but that bastard always found a way to pissed me off. I don't like what he said about you. His words ticked me off and I just had to punch him."

I palmed his cheek and kissed his lip, "Thank you for defending me. You did the right thing babe." I said.

"Of course I would defend you. No one talks shit about my girl." William said before taking my hand, "Let's go and find Noah."

We walked around and found Noah with William's parents.

"Mommy!" Noah screamed a ran to hug me. I picked up Noah and hug him back tightly.

"Oh my god, William! Jane! Are you two okay?" Carol came to us while panicking with Wade beside her.

"I'm sorry. That wasn't meant to happened. I tried not to get physical but he was pissing me off so bad." William told his parents.

"I warned you that Schmidt was no good. Have you ever listened to me son? Never get involved with people like him!" Wade exclaimed.

Carol narrowed her eyes towards Wade, "Stop it hun, it's over now."

"No Carol you don't get it. William out of all people should have know not to get involved with Sullivan Schmidt! Sullivan was bad, he would seek revenge! Who knew he would actually sabotage us and make the company went bankrupt. William should have think this all through." Somehow, Wade's words sounds too real to be true. What if Sullivan was really that bad and would actually seek revenge on William for humiliating him?

"Dad. I can handle it okay? Don't worry, I will make sure no want sabotage us and the company won't go bankrupt." William said, sighing.

"Alright, alright. Calm down, we still have an event going on right now. Let's not create anymore chaos okay?" Carol said, finally calming us all.

I sat on the chair with Noah in my lap. "Mommy, are you okay? Is daddy okay?" Noah asked.

"We're okay baby." I replied softly.

"I'm scared mommy." Noah said, eyes almost brimming in tears.

I pulled Noah to my chest and hug him closer to me. "You don't have to be scared now. Mommy is here with you okay."

"Don't leave me mommy." Noah pleaded.

"Baby, I will never leave you. You are my life. I can never live without you." I cooed.

Noah looked up at me and smile. "Okay. I love you mommy."

"I love you too sweetheart." I said and kissed his temple.

"Is Noah okay?" William asked me.

I nodded. "He's okay now."

I saw William checked his Rolex wristwatch and then looked at me.

"Hey, it's almost 10 pm. We have some important announcement to make. You will have to join me on the stage." William told me. "And bring Noah as well."

Suddenly, I froze and I can feel myself getting nervous. "William, can you at least tell me what's the important announcement?" I asked.

"Relax babe. I just wanted to introduce you and Noah to everyone." William said. "And one more thing, I hope after whatever happened tonight won't change what you feel towards me because I still love you with all my life."

I smiled at William. "Oh, okay then. Of course I still love you too William." I looked at the camera on my phone to check on my appearance. Then, I hold Noah's hand and we both followed William to the stage. There was an on-stage stands microphone in the middle of the stage.

William went to the microphone with me and Noah standing besides him. "Good evening ladies and gentlemen. First of all, I wanted to thank you all for being here tonight and I am truly sorry for the chaos that happened. Hopefully, you can still enjoy tonight's event. As you may know, I have an important announcement to make. Firstly, standing beside me tonight is my lovely girlfriend, Jane, and our wonderful son, Noah." he said while pointing at us. I smiled brightly and nodded towards the audience while squeezing Noah's shoulder.

"Secondly, this is dedicated to my wonderful Jane." William said and turned to look at me with an adoring smile that I love so much. "I know our first meeting was not how we wanted it to be. Regardless, I'm more than thankful to know you and have you in my life. My life has been better after you and Noah came in the picture. I want you to know that I will do anything to make you and Noah happy. So I really hope you will give me a chance and let me take care and love you both forever, for the rest of my life." My heart was beating so fast and tears brimmed in my eyes as I heard the audience gasped, seeing William get down on one knee, holding out a sparkling diamond ring.

"Jane Rosenfeld, will you marry me?"

In no cue, tears pouring down my face like a pouring rain as I nodding my head up and down repeatedly, "Yes William! Yes!" I answered with happy tears.

William put on the ring on my finger and he kiss me passionately in front of the clapping audience.

He broke off the kiss and picked up Noah in his arms. "Daddy and mommy is going to get married. I can finally officially be your dad, bud!"

Noah only laughed as he put his little hands around William's neck and hug him. "Yay for daddy!"

I joined their hug as well and right there on the stage, we had a family hug with everyone's still watching. But I don't really mind the attention, the sound of cameras flashing, reporters throwing questions and congratulations or even the accident that happened tonight. Because at the time, my mind was finally in ease and my heart is bursting out in happiness being in the warm, loving embrace of my fiancé and my son.

IS IT TOO SOON TO DO THIS YET? CAUSE I KNOW THAT IT'S DELICATE. ISN'T IT ISN'T IT ISN'T IT!!!!!!!!!!!!!!!!

you guys have to listen to delicate by taylor swift, i recommend it 1300000% <3

p.s if you already forgot about Sullivan, you can find him back on chapter 15!

i tried to write this chapter longer and write out the details very well but i was so tired, it took me hours to finished it (with a 15 mins break), so this is the best i could come out with for now. i was thinking of rewriting a new better version of this book BUT that's for the future. in the meantime, let's finish this book first shall we ;)

your votes and comments makes me so happy so please make the 'star' orange and leave as many comments as you can! :))

please VOTE, COMMENT AND FOLLOW!

Chapter 25

I JUST REALIZED THAT THIS BOOK HAVE LESS THAN 10 CHAPTERS LEFT!!!!

put on your seat belt people, this chapter is going to be a looong ride!

use your superhuman power to make the 'star' orange!!! ;)

enjoy reading :)

Jane's POV

It's finally weekend. The warm summer breeze, combined with the crisp, refreshing smells of the waterfront created a perfect day for sightseeing or just relaxing.

I was sitting on a garden chair at the beautifully decorated patio. I don't see William as someone that enjoys gardening but there was a small garden in the patio. William must be having it for planting pots with fruits, vegetables, blooming flowers, shrubs and possibly even trees. William must have hired a garden and landscape designer to design a stunning outdoor space for his patio. With a petite patch of green, the creative planters and unique ideas here can easily make the garden fit for a king.

I flip over the pages of the Food Network Magazine that I'm currently reading, trying to find some new recipes for me to learn. Other than dancing, I also enjoy cooking and baking. Now that we have a big kitchen with complete kitchen supplies, my urge to cook has just getting bigger. William has told me that we could have just hired a maid to cook for us. But in my opinion, what's the point of having a nice, big kitchen if we never use it and only let the maid do the work? Where's the fun in that? Besides, Noah much more preferred my cooking. Luckily, after a while, William also has became more fond of my cooking too.

This morning, I made the classic french toast. I found out that Noah actually likes to eat french toast with peanut butter on top. Meanwhile, William and me preferred french toast with warm mapple syrup. Other than french toast, I also made cheesy chicken omelette which I learned from the Food Network Magazine. It's nothing fancy, just a fantastic basic cheese omelette with chicken slice. They taste great together in this big, flavor-packed omelette.

I'm still sitting on the garden chair in the patio, reading the food recipe magazine when I heard the sound of footsteps nearing me.

"Hey love." William called me.

"Hey" I replied without looking, my eyes were still fixed to the magazine in front of me.

He came up behind me and started rubbing my shoulders. "What are you reading babe?" he asked me while taking a peak at the magazine.

I flipped the pages of the Food Network Magazine. "It's just a food magazine with recipes. I'm trying to learn some new recipes. See, this one looks good right?" I asked him, pointing at a page that showed a black pepper chicken fried steak with fries and salad.

"Mmm, looks delicious." he replied, rubbing my shoulders a bit more before running his hands down toward my breasts. I was stunned and froze.

"William." I moaned.

"Yes baby?" he asked amusingly. He cupped my breasts in his hands and squeezed it gently.

My head leaned back. "Babe, what are you doing?" I whispered frantically.

William chuckled and squeezed my breasts a little harder.

"Argh!" my voice came out in a little squeak.

William let go of my breasts while laughing at me. "Sorry babe." he said.

I huffed, faking to sulk in anger. "Stop teasing me, will you?"

"Alright, I'm sorry honey. It's just that, you looked so tense. I'm trying to help you let loose and chill." he said, chuckling.

"I'm totally fine. I need no chill because I am very much chill okay." I told him with a strong emphasis on the word 'very'.

William only chuckled and smirked at me. Color rushed to my cheeks when his eyes sparkling in amusement.

"Right, fine. You are so chill, I get it." he let out a small laugh.

"Stop laughing!" I told him.

As much as I was annoyed by his sneaky and playful behavior, it was actually moments like this that makes me happy. Sometimes we acted childishly towards each other and William just love to tease me on every chances he got. Even worse when Noah teamed up with William to tease or prank me. But deep in my heart, I know that the small, happy moments like this is what I live for.

"Alright! I'll stop, I'll stop." William squealed at me. "Okay. Listen babe. I have something to tell you. Actually, I have some surprises for you."

I looked at William curiously, raising my eyebrows at him. "Surprises? What kind of surprise? It's not even my birthday, you know that right."

"Yeah I know when is your birthday but that's not the point. Now come on, I want you to come with me. I have two surprises for you. I'm going to show you the first surprise." he told me while holding out his hand for me to take.

I don't know if I should be nervous or excited. This is all very sudden to me I can't even comprehend it. Despite the nervousness, I took his hand and follow him anyway.

William took me inside and then lead me to the front door.

We were now standing behind the closed front door. "Okay, I want you to close your eyes for me." William told me.

"What? No! Just tell me what it is." I shrieked.

"But it's a surprise! Oh come on, just close your eyes for me babe." he pleaded.

"Ugh fine. Only because I think you're cute." I muttered under my breath and close my eyes. Now I'm getting more suspicious at what the surprise is going to be.

I heard William opened the front door. My grip of his hand becomes tighter as he lead me outside. After a few steps later, we finally stopped.

"Okay, you can open your eyes now." William told me.

I was shaking as I slowly opened my eyes and adjusted to the surrounding. Then, I realized that we were at the car porch. That was when I saw a brand new, black Audi A8 parked in the car porch, right in front of me.

"What the-" I gasped, shocked.

It can't be.

"YOU BOUGHT ME A CAR?" I asked, or maybe it sounded more like I shouted. Or screamed.

William grin widely at me. "Yes babe. Do you like it?"

"Do I like it? I love it, Will! Oh my god I love it so much!" I screamed excitedly.

"Well, I'm glad you love it. I know you have always wanted to have your own car and besides, having a car will make it easier for you to go anywhere. So I figured, why not buy you a car." William explained while smiling at me.

My eyes brimmed with happy tears. "I can't believe this. Oh my god baby, thank you so much!" I jumped and hug him tightly.

"Don't thank me babe. You deserves it." William said while hugging me back.

I pulled away from the hug then put my hands around his neck and kiss him on the lips.

"You are the best boyfriend ever!" I exclaimed.

William raised his eyebrows at me, "Babe," he whined. "You may want to correct that, cuz I'm your fiancé babe, fiancé!" he exasperated.

I gasped. "Oh. My. God. Fiancé. We're engaged a-and oh my god you are my fiancé!"

"Really babe? You forgot that we already engaged?" William asked playfully.

"No! I'm sorry, it's just that... it still haven't sink in yet that we're engaged now." I told him. "But babe, thank you so much. I still can't believe it that you bought me a car! An Audi to be exact!" I exclaimed with much excitement.

William laughed and kissed my forehead. "Anything for my lady."

I looked up at William. "Will, you said there are two surprises. What is the other surprise?" I asked curiously, excited to know what is waiting for me.

William put a hand behind his neck sheepishly. "Well, do you remember when you told me that you wanted to see your dad again?" he asked.

"Um yeah, why?" I asked, curiosity getting the best of me.

"Okay so I thought why not we all go and visit him. What do you think?" William told me.

My eyes widen. "You wanted to come along? You want to see my dad? Honey... oh god, really? Are you sure?" I asked question after question.

"Yeah, I mean why not, right? I'm sure Noah would want to see his other grandad too." William said.

"You're right. But when can we go?" I asked with hopeful eyes.

"Since it's weekend and I don't have to work today so, what if we go today? As in right now?" said William.

"Today? Like right now?" I asked him. "I mean sure. But I gotta go change! And oh, I gotta tell Noah too!" I said frantically.

William put his hands on my shoulder. "Hey, relax. Everything's good okay. You go tell Noah and change. I'm going to warm up the car while waiting for you."

I took a deep breath and exhaled. "Alright. I'm good, all good."

I swiftly sprinted inside, searching for Noah. Finally, I found him playing with his toys in the playroom.

"Hey sweetie." I said.

Noah looked up to me from his toys. "Mommy!"

"Baby, I need you to go and change your clothes. We're going out today." I told Noah.

Noah looked at me curiously with his big doe eyes. "Where are we going mommy?"

I looked at Noah softly and gave him a warm smile. "Oh honey, we're going to see your grandad."

-

It turns out that my dad's house-my old home, was not really far from the penthouse. It took only 15 or 20 minutes to arrive at my dad's place. We have parked in the driveway. My dad's classic, old light brown Volkswagen GTI was also parked in the driveway, meaning he was home.

I looked outside to the front porch through the car window. I looked around, try to find any glimpse of my dad but the house was too quite, so lonely. Is this really how it has been like since I left? Now I feel even more bad and guilty for leaving my dad alone.

I feel William squeezed my hands that was constantly fiddling on my lap, "You okay?" he asked.

"Yeah I'm fine. It's just that, this brings back so many memories. The good ones and the bad ones." I told him sincerely.

He slightly rubbed the back of my hand with his thumb. "Stay calm. That's okay, we can go inside whenever you're ready."

I took a deep breath. "I think I'm ready. Let's go."

William nodded. We both get out from the car after William turned off the engine. I opened the back door of the vehicle and unbuckled Noah from the seat belt.

"Whose house is this mommy?" Noah asked me as I helped him with his struggle to get out from the car.

"My dad's house. Which is your grandpa, sweetie." I told him.

Noah's eyes widen. "Why don't we live here before? Why you never bring me here mommy?" he asked.

I sighed. "It's a long story, baby. Now let's get inside and meet your grandpa first okay? Aren't you excited?"

Noah jumped and smile sweetly at me, showing his teeth. "I can't wait to meet grandpa! Do you think grandpa will love me mommy? Will he play with me?"

"Of course sweetheart. You are his only grandson. I'm sure he'll love you just as much as I do." I said, hoping that it's true.

William looked at us. "You two ready?"

"I'm ready! I'm ready!" Noah exclaimed.

I chuckled at Noah's excitement. "Yeah, we're ready." Or so I hope.

We stood at the front door. William was waiting for me to make the first move. My hands are shaking, my heart beats so fast I think it's going to explode and then I'm probably going to die right at this very front door of my old home. That doesn't sound like a pleasant way to die.

I looked at the buzzer-doorbell, next to the front door. Never onced in my life that I have to used it to get inside. Usually, I already have the key to get in or my mom or dad will open it. Unlike the penthouse, William has setup a buzzer type system. Us, owners, opened the front door by inserting an electronic key. Meanwhile, visitors will have to press a buzzer next to the front door then spoke into a microphone to request the owner to let them get in.

I took a deep breath and counted to three. I saw the buzzer next to the door and pressed it. I was becoming nervous so I mentally counted to three again in my head.

I heard footsteps from the inside. This is it. There's no turning back now. I have to face it either way, it's now or never. I heard some shuffling and then I heard the sound of the doorknob being twist.

The front door was being opened, making a creaking sound due to its old condition. There he stood on the doorway was none other than my dad. He looked a bit pale and his hair is shorter. His body was hunched but he still stand tall, eyes sparkling with determined face. My dad was wearing his typical faded blue jeans with a dark green tshirt. As I scanned his face, I realized that he hasn't changed so much else than his hair was a little bit shorter now.

His eyes raked from me to William and lastly to Noah. "J-Jane?" he asked in a raspy and strained voice. I have no idea why his voice sounded like that, either he hasn't been drinking enough water and he had a sore throat or he just haven't been saying or calling my name in a while now.

It took me a while to respond. I was pulled back to reality when William nudge me on the shoulder. Before I could even reply, Noah cut in before me.

"Are you my grandpa?" Noah asked my dad. He is usually scared of strangers but he doesn't seemed so scared of my dad.

My dad looked towards Noah, "Grandpa? Y-you're my grandson?" he stuttered, shocked.

"Dad," I called for him. "Yes it's me Jane. This is my fiancé, William." I pointed to William. "And this is my, uh, son." I pointed to Noah.

"Hello grandpa! My name is Noah." Noah said excitedly, introducing himself to my dad.

"Oh dear. Jane, it's really you? My daughter!" my dad exclaimed. Tears brimmed in his eyes, he looks like he was about to cry anytime soon and so do I.

"Yes dad. It is me. It's really me." I said, sobbing. I couldn't hold my tears anymore as it poured down my face.

"Jane! Oh my god! You're back. My daughter is safe and she's back!" my dad said, his voice filled with relieve. "Oh sweetheart, come here. I was worried about you almost everyday. I missed you Jane." my dad told me as he pulled me into a warm hug. I hugged him back tightly. I miss being so close to him. I can smell the familiar scent of my dad, and it smell like home.

"Dad, I'm so sorry. I'm so so sorry." I cried out. "I'm sorry. I'm sorry. I missed you more dad. I'm really sorry." I don't know how many times I have repeated the word 'sorry' to my dad but no matter how much it still won't be enough. I feel emotionally drained. I can't believe I still get to hold my dad again, I thought this day will never come.

"Honey, stop saying sorry. I have forgiven you long ago. Just promise me you won't leave again. You're the only family I have after your mother is gone, Jane." my dad told me, his voice sounding sad and vulnerable.

I looked into my dad's eyes, "I won't disappeare again dad, I promise."

"Thank god Jane. Alright, let's go inside. Bring your uh... bring them inside." my dad said, looking at William and Noah.

I nodded with a smile.

We all step inside and I instantly feel warm. The warmth reminds me of my teenage years, that I've spent in this house. I looked at the hangin pictures on the wall as I walked through the hallway. There's a picture of a 6-year-old me and then there's a picture of me playing on the swing with my mom beside me. Lastly, I saw our family photo. I traced the photo lightly with my hand, thinking that one day I will have my own family photo with William and Noah.

My dad looked at William. "Come on. Have a sit and get comfortable, I'll go get some drinks." he said. "Oh man, I don't usually treat the guests. That used to be my wife's job." he chuckled.

"It's fine. Don't worry Mr. Rosenfeld, you don't have to get us anything." William replied to my dad as he sit on the couch with Noah.

My dad stand still with his hands on his hips. "It won't be a trouble William. Oh and please, call me David."

"Dad, why don't you sit with them and maybe have a talk? Don't worry, I'll go make some tea." I offered.

"But you don't-"

I cut off my dad, "Dad. I know where everything was placed at. I used to live here too remember?"

My dad was in his thought. "Oh, right. Yeah, alright. You go make some tea then." he said and took a seat at the armchair.

I chuckled and went to the kitchen as I heard my dad and William started talking. William is much better at having a conversation than me, probably because he has been doing that with his clients. He has to do a lot of presentations and give speeches at a every formal event that he attend.

I poured down the boiling water and took out a tea bag. I add some sugar and stir the tea. I was pouring the tea into each of the tea cups when I heard some laughter erupted from the living room. Well, at least they get along so well.

I put all the tea cups on the cream colored tray and bring it to the living room. "Here's the tea." I said as I put the tray on the coffee table.

"Thanks babe." William said.

"Ah, thank you Jane. I missed having the drink you made. You used to make my coffee. Oh William, this girl right here made the best coffee in the whole wide world, I tell you." my dad exclaimed.

My cheeks turned red. "Dad! It was just coffee." I whined.

William laughed. "Oh yes. She is the best cooker too." William said while smirking at me.

They both laughed.

"I love chicken nuggets." Noah suddenly chirped in. "Mommy makes the best chicken nuggets!" he exclaimed.

I went to sit besides Noah and ruffles his hair.

"Oh look at you handsome boy. Is this the precious little Noah?" my dad raised his eyebrows at me.

I nodded, "Yeah."

"Very well. Hello Noah, I'm grandpa David. Come here dear." my dad said to Noah.

Noah jumped out from the couch and went to sit on my dad's lap.

"Grandpa? Do you have any story?" Noah asked.

"Story huh... I think I do have one." my dad said, his eyes filled with warmth.

"Tell me, grandpa! Tell me! Tell me!" Noah said excitedly.

"Alright, alright. Oh boy, here we go..." my dad started telling his made up story to Noah. My heart warms looking at the scene. William put a hand around my shoulder and hug me.

"I told you everything's going to be fine." he whispered to me. I can only nodded at his words, still mesmerized by the natural affectionate bond between my dad and Noah.

While my dad was still busy telling stories at Noah, I slowly make myself upstairs with William followed behind me. Thousands of memories came rushing back to me as I entered my old room. This is where I grew up.

"Hmm, young Jane was very, girly." William chuckled as he looked around my room. The walls are light pink. I have some typical cartoon and band posters taped on the wall. I also used to own many pink diaries, sparkling hair clips and glitters. That was all from my childhood years. During my teenage years, I kept black sweatshirts and collect poems and mixtapes. Or as the people would call, the emo phase.

"Not really." I said. All my things are still in its place. Nothing have been touched, yet there's no dust anywhere. Dad must have cleaned my room sometimes. How thoughtful of him. Or maybe he just missed me. The thought of him cleaning my room, all alone, sadly looking through my things, made me frown.

"You have a nice home." William told me as he join to sit beside me on my bed.

"Yeah, you could say that." I agreed."Sometimes I wonder why do I even ran away. I have a nice home and a loving dad. It's not like my dad has kicked me out. Running away from home was probably my biggest mistake." I sighed.

William took my chin in his hand and tilted my head so I could look at him in the eyes. "Jane, don't say that. Try to think in a positive way. If you haven't ran away, then we probably wouldn't have met. Don't you think? So that's probably not a mistake."

"You're right, but-"

William shake his head, "You being with that prick Adam was a mistake. You're not supposed to willingly gave yourself at him."

I looked at William, the thought of Adam really seemed to made him angry. "But William, without Adam I wouldn't have Noah. And I most probably never thought Noah as a mistake. I want him, I love him. He's my first baby that I ever carried. So me being with Adam is not a mistake. It was just me being a fool and stupid enough to trust Adam. But I have learned my lesson now. And besides, I have you now." I said, smiling softly at William.

William nodded his head knowingly, "Yeah. So there's no mistake, really. It's just like a... beautiful disaster."

"Beautiful disaster?" I questioned him.

"Yup. Because every disaster that you did, that happened, every results came out beautifully. I mean, you get Noah, then you met me.

So you see, it's a beautiful disaster." William told me. He cupped my cheeks and kissed me slowly and passionately on the lips.

"Mhm, you're right." I whispered.

After the little talk with William, we go back downstairs to see my dad just finished telling his stories to Noah.

"Mommy, daddy! Grandpa told me a dinosaur story. He told me dinosaur was real." Noah exclaimed.

"Oh no, is that true? Do you want to tell me the story that grandpa has told you?" William bend down to picked up Noah in his arms.

William looked at me and nodded his head towards my dad, as if he was telling me to talk to my dad privately. I smiled, silently thanked him.

I slowly went to sit on the couch. "Hey dad. I hope Noah was being good with you."

"Oh that boy. He can be sneaky, indeed, but he was really smart too. You made the right choice of keeping him, Jane."

I sighed. "Oh dad, I'm really sorry for what I did. I regret it as soon as I left. But I'm very thankful to have William with me. He was really nice."

I saw my dad eyeing the engagement ring on my finger. "Oh and uh, he proposed to me weeks ago. So we're engaged now. I think he is the one. He loves Noah and Noah loves him too so I figured why not saying yes to his proposal."

My dad smile brightly. "I can't believe it. My daughter is finally engaged to a nice man. And you didn't tell me he was a billionaire!

I have to figured it out myself when I asked him what he did for a living. He's a CEO!" my dad exclaimed.

I smiled sheepishly. "Oh yeah, about that huh. Well yeah, he was a player but he's a really changed man now, dad. I mean, he proposed to me and we're engaged now. So he must really love me right."

"Sure he loves you. I just hope he would stay like that until after marriage." my dad sighed.

I frowned. "Dad."

"I'm sorry Jane. I just, I don't want you to get hurt again. It hurts me too. I promised your mom I would take care of you. I don't want William to be just like Adam, used you then throw you away." my dad's angry face now turned to sad. "Oh Jane if only you knew, ever since your mother is gone, I've been living my whole damn life to see you-my little girl, smile. Sweetheart, I didn't bring you up so guys like Adam could wear you down. I live my life only to see you smile and make you happy, so please don't let nobody take that away."

I was sobbing the whole time my dad was talking. He continued, "No one knows but, it nearly killed me the day they put your mom in the ground. The only thing that kept me alive was seeing you smile. I can't bear losing you too."

I hug my dad and put my head on his chest. He rubs my back gently.

"When you left, I really thought it was the end. I really thought I was going to lose you forever. Your mom once said to me, one day you will grow up and do silly and stupid things. But no matter what you did, she told me to always forgive, not punish. Then you will grow and learn your mistake. She was right all along. As if she could see it coming." my dad chuckled.

"Thank you dad. You are really the best dad ever. I love you." I said, my eyes red from crying.

My dad kissed the temple of my head, "I love you too Jane. You'll always be my little girl." he replied.

After spending some more time, it was finally time for us to go home.

"When you're here again, we can draw dinosaurs together yeah." my dad told Noah.

"Okay grandpa. I will bring my dinosaur toy too, daddy bought it for me!" Noah replied.

"Alright dad, we'll visit you again soon. I love you, and take care!" I told my dad and kissed him on the cheek.

"Sure sweetheart. Just call me if you need anything." he said and then turned to Wiliam. "I hope you take a really good care of my daughter and my grandson."

William shake his head up and down repeatedly. "Yes, David. I will love them with all my heart. And please take care of yourself too. Jane was always worried about you."My dad laughed, "Oh don't worry about this old man. I might be old but I'm still strong."

We all laughed. After bidding goodbye, we finally make our way home. I'm so happy everything went smoothly.

"Thank you William. Thank you for the surprise. You made me the happiest girl today. I can't believe I finally get to see my dad again. I had such a good time." I told Wiliam and smiled.

"Anything for you. If you're happy, then I'm happy." he said. "I'm glad you finally settled things down with your dad."

I nodded, "Yeah, I was glad for that too. And I'm also far than happy that your parents can accept me and Noah. Especially your mom, she was really nice." That is true though, Carol has greeted me with opened arms and a warm hug. She is definitely not like other rich people who only socialize with elite people like her. Carol was a lot more nicer. "Thanks, I love you Will."

"Sure, I love you too." he said while squeezing my hand.

Everything has finally fall into place. Everyone's happy and everything's perfect. But somehow, even after all this happiness we're having, I can't help but have a bad feeling.

My guts could be wrong, but again, I had a really bad feeling. I hope I was wrong. It could either be nothing... or everything.

DUN DUN DUNNNNN

i take this chapter seriously and should i say emotionally too? because i cried along with jane on david's words. "The only thing that kept me alive was seeing you smile." :'(

please VOTE, COMMENT AND FOLLOW!

Chapter 26

Jane's POV

The day was hot and sunny. I noticed that I have been sweating a lot lately. I've been sweating the whole time that I have finally came up with a conclusion that I don't feel like wearing anything right now but that would be inappropriate since Noah is also at home with me. Luckily William is at work, I don't think he would like to see me in a sweaty mess like this. But I'm sure he doesn't mind to see me naked though.

I'm sure it's not just my imagination anymore. This year has actually been abnormally hot so far. No doubt that I am getting a bit worried with the hot weather because I've read an article somewhere that researchers actually expected this year to be cooler than the previous year.

I am now wearing a thin green shirt with a loose pants. My body was so sweaty that it made my clothes stick to my skin like a second layer.

I looked at the sight of my boy, Noah, chalking on his easel. His worn out shirt was splattered with various paints of green, blue, red and yellow. William has bought him a brand new watercolor paint set. Noah has taken his sweet time to paint using his new painting set and now he has switched to the colorful chalks and easel for some chalking.

Having a three year old boy like Noah, I am always looking for something to play, learn, and also some creative and imaginative activities for us to do.

Don't judge me, I do love arts and paintings but sometimes I just hate paints because of the mess. Somehow, on this very sunny day, we take the paints outside. I put Noah in old clothes and it doesn't matter if he makes a mess as I get him cleaned up before we go inside.

"Mommy look," Noah called out for me. I walked over to him, smiling brightly while looking at the easel. There were three stick figures holding hands drawn on the easel.

"Ohh, what did you draw honey?" I asked sweetly.

Noah pointed at the first figure. "This is you mommy," His finger shifted to the next stick figure which is a lot smaller. "And this is me!"

"Aw that is so sweet. What about the last one?" I asked.

"This tall man here is daddy." Noah giggled.

I smiled and clapped my hands, "That's very nice baby!"

Noah gave a fake curtsy. "I can't wait to show this to daddy. Mommy, do you think daddy will love this?" Noah asked with a pout.

"Sweetie, of course daddy would love this. He would be so proud of you Noah. This is the first and the cutest portrait of our family ever!" I exclaimed. I kissed him on the forehead and ruffled his hair.

"Thank you mommy. From now on, I want to draw and paint more things! When I grow up, I can sell my drawings and become rich like daddy! Right mommy?" Noah asked with a hopeful glint in his eyes.

I laughed and shook my head, "Sure honey, but you need to fix your drawing and painting skill a little if you want to be able to sell your paintings."

Noah frowned but then a smile slowly crept onto his face. "Okay mommy. I promise, I will practice to draw everyday so I can sell my painting and make you proud."

I looked at Noah lovingly. What did I do to deserve him? Noah is such a nice kid and I am more than grateful to have him as my son.

I put my hands on Noah's shoulder and look at him in the eyes, "Love, you already made me happy and proud of you. I just hope that one day you will grow up becoming a good man that knows how to treat people fairly and nicely." My eyes brimmed with tears. "I promise baby, I will try to be the best mom for you and make you happy. I won't let you down. I love you so much." I said with a sad smile.

Noah nodded his head repeatedly and put his hand on my cheek. He wiped a tear from the side of my face gently with his small dainty hand.

"Don't cry mommy. I love you and daddy too. Always!" Noah said and went forward to kiss me on the cheek.

I chuckled at the little boy, "Alright, alright. Come on big guy, let's go inside and get you clean up. Then, we can make pancakes together!"

"Pancakes!" Noah exclaimed and swiftly ran inside while struggling to get out from his messy shirt. I laughed at the sight of my little boy.

-

"No honey don't-!" I said, diving for Noah's arm, but I was too late. Me and Noah were baking chocolate muffins for William.

"Why mommy?" Noah asked with a shocked face.

I sighed, "Oh Noah. We're not supposed to add the chocolate chip yet. We need to apply the icing first."

Noah looked at me with a guilty face but managed to smile sheepishly at me, "I'm sorry mommy. But why can't we put the chocolate chip first?"

"Noah, now how are we going to apply the icing? Over the chocolate chips? It's going to look ugly!" I snapped.

Noah dropped the chocolate chip on the counter. He put his head down and look at his feet and at the floor. I can see a little pout forming on his lower lip.

I looked at Noah and sigh. Now I feel bad for snapping at him. I rarely scold him, I don't usually have to raise my voice and use my motherly tone on him since he was always a good kid. I don't even know what is wrong with me these last few days. A week after visiting my dad, I started feeling unusually fatigue which includes headaches and back pains. But the worst to top it all is probably mood swings. I get annoyed easily, get mad easily and even get over excited sometimes. I still remember that one night when William decided to order pizzas, 3 boxes of pizza, and I can't stop smiling because of it. I blame my mood swings on all those sleepless nights that I had.

I kneel down on Noah's level and slowly lifted his chin so he would look at me.

I caressed his cheek with my hand, "Sweetie. I'm sorry, I didn't mean to snap at you." I continued to stroke his cheek tenderly. "Honey, you know what? It doesn't matter if we put the icing or the chocolate chip first. It would still tastes good."

Noah looked at me with tears brimming in his eyes, "But you said it would look ugly. Daddy is going to hate it when it is ugly."

I kissed his forehead and look at him while smiling, "Honey, I'm sure daddy will love it. Trust me." I said. Noah seems uncertain of my answer. "Well, what if we don't put the icing? Besides, I think daddy is not really a big fan of frosting anyway." I shrugged.

"Really mommy? Okay, no frosting for daddy then." Noah said with a grin.

"Alright sweetie." I kissed him on the forehead again before embracing him in a hug. "Now baby, will you do the honor to help me decorate these muffins?" I asked.

"Yes, your majesty." Noah replied with a giggle.

We continue to decorate the muffins for another hour. I looked at the clock and realized that it was already evening and the weather is getting hotter outside.

I turned my head to look at Noah and gasp, "Noah, stop it!" I shouted playfully while grabbing the muffins away from him. We have finally finished baking our famous chocolate muffins and have successfully decorated it with some sprinkles and chocolate chips. We were supposed to wait until William is home so that we could all eat it together. Apparently Noah had a different idea when I have caught him almost eating one of the muffins.

"But mommy... it looks so yummy and so pretty. I want to eat it now!" he whined.

"Sweetie, you can eat it when daddy's home later. Just a few hours, it won't be long." I told Noah.

"But I want it now! I want it now!" he whined again.

I looked at Noah with a stern face but not too stern that he would think I was actually mad. "Noah..."

"But I made the muffins. It's my muffin. Mine." Noah huffed.

I chuckled and keep the muffins. "Don't worry little chef, trust me, it will be all worth it when we eat together later. Also, daddy will be sad if you don't wait for him."

"Fine, only because I love daddy." Noah mumbled as he walked out of the kitchen away from me and the delicious smelling and good looking muffins.

I heard the door to Noah's bedroom door being closed to signal that he was in his room. I quickly took the rag and rinse it with lukewarm water to wipe the counter. When I was about done cleaning the counter, I heard loud knocking came from the front door.

That was weird, I thought. Usually people would just ring the doorbell. I wash my hand clean and went to the living room. I turned my head slightly at the hallway and glad that Noah is still in his room.

I slowly make my way to the front door. The knocking at the door became harsher by seconds. I wonder who could it be.

I almost decided to call William but I don't want him to be worried since he is probably busy right now.

Once I reached the front door, I took a deep breath before asking, "Who's there?"

No answer.

Suddenly the person knocks at the door again, but it was calmer this time and not as harsh as before.

I decided to open the front door. I was expecting a familiar face but clearly not this one. Not him.

"Mr. Schmidt." I addressed him. He was alone. His face seemed pale and his eyes looked tired.

"Ah, Jane. Lovely to see you. Please, just call me Sullivan."

I scoffed.

"I'm sure you know that me and your fiancé are very close. Like brothers, you know?" he laughed.

"What are you doing here? What do you want Sullivan? William is not home." I told him intently.

That is probably my first mistake, to tell him that William isn't home and I was alone with my son with no one to protect us if the guy in front of me ever thought of hurting us right now.

Sullivan chuckled. "Pft, of course I know he isn't home. Otherwise, why would I be here right now?" he smirked. "I went to see him a few days ago, to maybe... you know... fix our alliance. But William and his ego, he kicked me out from his building again and even have the nerves to banned me. How dare he."

I straighten my posture and put on my poker face. "That is a problem between you and my fiancé. I have nothing to do with it. Now if you don't mind I have other important things to do."

Sullivan smirked and took a step closer to me. "Sweetheart, don't be so tough on me now. I'm just trying to be civilian here. I just want to be nice to you." He lifted a strand of my hair and sniffed it. It sent shiver throughout my body but not in a pleasuring way. "You're such a pretty lady, that bastard is so lucky but he didn't even know it."

I quickly push his chest, wanting him away from me. "You've crossed the line there. If you ever thought of disrespecting me again then I won't hesitate to file a restraining order against you. Please leave." I said contentedly.

Sullivan only smile slightly at me. "Alright. So you also wanna play it rough huh?" he took a step right in front of me while holding the door handle so hard I almost thought it would break.

Sullivan pushed the door roughly then gripped my arm so hard that I flinched. "I'm warning you woman, don't try to act so bitchy in front of me! And tell your so beloved fiancé that I will get him back for what he did. He better not try to do anything stupid if he knows that he couldn't handle the risk."

Sullivan let go of my arm and I stumbled a bit. I instantly rub my arm to soothe it. God, this man has a grip of a gorilla.

"If you didn't do anything stupid first then I can assure you that my fiancé wouldn't even think about it, not even in the slightest bit!" I said firmly.

Sullivan gave me a death stare before leaving.

Well that was surprising, who would have thought that I will be getting an unwelcome guest today.

Seeing that Sullivan has left, I hurriedly close the front door and went inside to check on Noah.

-----

i am truly sorry for the late update, i've been busy these past days so it's hard to finish even just a chapter :(honestly i'm not satisfied with this chapter & i don't like the ending. i wish i could write a little longer & make the sullivan part seem more threatening. don't blame me, when you're stressed it would be hard to get ideas or get inspired.

i'll be doing slow update so i want to thank everyone who are still reading this story. the time you spent to read this & also your votes are much appreciated.

please VOTE, COMMENT AND FOLLOW!

Chapter 27

Jane's POV

Everything feels wrong and I don't like it. After the threat that I got from Sullivan a few days ago, I haven't been the same. At least that's what William told me.

I have told William about the threat and he said not to worry, he will handle it. But I can't seem to sit still, thinking about all the possible thing that could happened.

And by following my motherly instinct, I constantly worried about Noah so here I am driving to my dad's house in my brand new car with Noah on the back seat.

I am going to drop off Noah at his granpa's house for a few days because that way he will be safer and out of Sullivan's reach.

I know I'm only being paranoid for thinking of the worst thing but I can't help it. It's a mother thing you know?

I haven't told William yet about sending Noah to my dad's place. I'm not sure what he would think about this and how he would react on my decision. If he thinks otherwise I'm just going to tell him that I'm only being careful and cautious.

There's nothing wrong on being extra careful right?

"Mommy, why do I have to stay at grandpa's?" Noah asked me.

I looked at him from the rear view mirror, "Why honey? Don't you want to spend a little time with your grandpa?"

"Yes I want. Mommy, do you think grandpa have more dinasaur stories to tell me?"

I glanced at Noah with a slight smirk. "Oh I'm sure he has. I called grandpa this morning and he told me he has so many things planned out for the two of you."

Noah's eyes widen and he held his hands up. "Yay! I can't wait to see grandpa."

"Sure sweetie, we'll be there soon." I chuckled.

Noah was fumbling with his toy for a while before asking, "Mommy, why don't I have a little brother? If I have a brother we can play together. It is no fun playing alone in the play room." he pouted.

I sighed. I never thought about having another child, at least not now. I feel bad after hearing Noah's words. I haven't thought about how Noah has been feeling. Of course he was lonely. He's turning 4 next year and still haven't had any friends.

I thought everything was fine. We would send Noah off to school when he's 4 and he would meet so many tiny people like him, make friends and draw together. But I never thought he would need a company now.

Maybe I should start talking about this with William. But what would he think? Do he wants children with me?

My thought was cut off by Noah's loud voice shrieking, "Mommy!"

"Yes honey? I'm sorry, I'm driving right now you see?" I said sheepishly.

"Mommy, I am asking you. Can I have a brother? Please." Noah pleaded.

"Yes baby, anything for you sweetheart." I said, though I'm not entirely convinced with my reply.

Noah grin widely and clap his hands, "Yay! I will have friends to play with at home!"

I looked at Noah from the rear view mirror and smile fondly at him.

After a while, we finally arrived at my dad's house. I parked the car and hurried to get Noah out of the car since he was very eager and excited to see his grandpa again.

I saw my dad standing at the front door to greet us. "Hello my favorite boy!"

Noah sprint towards my dad and jump into his arms. "Hello grandpa! I miss you!"

"Smart boy, I miss you too." my dad replied, grinning widely.

"Hi dad," I smile, feeling warm and happy looking at my son easily getting attached to his grandpa. "How are you?" I asked my dad.

"Sweet Jane, I'm always fine right here. How are you doing? And where's William?" my dad asked as we all walked inside to the living room.

Noah was quick to sit on the floor and switched the TV to a familiar cartoon show. My dad and I sit on the couch while smiling at the sight of Noah eagerly watching his cartoon show.

"I'm alright dad. Just been tired lately." I said, not mentioning about the threat because I don't want him to worry about me. "William's at work."

"You do look tired and a bit pale. Are you sure you're alright? See the doctor if you feel anything strange." my dad told me.

"I will dad." I said, shaking my head slightly at my dad for being overprotective as always.

"Are you sure it's okay for me to drop Noah here for a few days? Don't you have anything to do?" I asked.

My dad shrugged, "It's fine Jane. Noah is my grandson, you can drop him here anytime. Besides, I take some days off from work. Wanna spend some time with my boy."

I smiled. "Thanks dad. He's a good kid so I bet he won't ask for a lot of things."

"Oh shush. Even if he ask for a green tea flavored ice cream, I would do anything to get it for him." my dad said.

We both laughed. "Oh dad please. But you're lucky because Noah won't ask for that kind of stuff. Green tea is not his thing." I said, chuckling.

I looked at the hanging clock on the wall and realized that it was almost 6. William will be back from work soon. He will get worried if he finds out I'm not home.

"Dad, I gotta go. William will be back soon." I told him while getting up from the couch.

"Leaving already? I'm sure William wouldn't mind you spend some more time here." said my dad.

I sighed, "Sorry dad. I would love to stay but I got a dinner to prepare at home. See you in a few days. Love you dad." I said while hugging my dad.

"I love you sweetheart." my dad replied. "Noah, your mommy is leaving, say bye."

Noah turned to look at me and quickly ran to hug me. "I love you mommy."

"I love you too sweetie. So so much. Mommy will come back in a few days to take you home okay? Stay here and be a good boy to grandpa." I told Noah and kissed his cheek a few times.

I went inside my car and swiftly drove back to the penthouse.

-

William's POV

It's been a long day at work and it's safe to say that I am pleased to see the end of my working hour and eager to get home to see my beloved fiancée, Jane.

We have been together for quite a while now but these past few days she has been a little distant with me. For instance, when I try to wrap my arms around her waist when I hug her, she slowly whined she's tired and not in the mood then slowly tugs herself away.

Is she getting bored of me? Does she not love me anymore?

I know deep down that I am still utterly in love with Jane Rosenfeld, from the way her nose crinkles when she laughs, to how when we watch a movie together she's so interested in what's happening but I can't help but stare at how beautiful she is as I admire her features.

Maybe she's just worried too much about Sullivan. That prick, I should have just killed him for having the nerve to come over at my place and talked to my girl. I'm so mad that I wasn't there when Sullivan came.

I know that I have been working for extra hours lately but I don't really mind because I know at the end it will all be worth it if it means I get to see Jane and my little boy Noah smile a real genuine smile with their eyes glittering with joy.

HONK

HONK

HONK

I was knocked out of my thoughts by the amplifying sound of vibrations from the car behind me. I raised my hands in an apologetic manor before taking off in the direction of Jane and I's penthouse.

A millionaire getting honked? Now that's a first. I chuckled slightly.

"Jane, I'm home!" I shout through the empty living room, not receiving the usual "in here babe" from Jane and followed by Noah's adorable giggles.

I got worried and started to search for Jane. Taking off my suit and setting my keys down on the cabinet beside the door, I slowly make my way to the kitchen to see if my pretty girl is at the kitchen island preparing dinner as per usual.

A frown evident on my face when I notice that Jane isn't where I expected to be with panic rising as I continued to look for her.

"Babe this isn't funny. Where are you? Noah, buddy?" Still no response as I decided on walking up the stairs to search for Jane and Noah.

I heard some shuffling from our bedroom. I quickly make my way inside to see Jane just got out from the adjoining bathroom in just her white towel covering her body.

I strode over to her and brought my large hands up to her cheeks leaning down to her, after a while of watching Jane closing her eyes in anticipation, I finally put my warm lips to her soft ones.

I pulled away staring at Jane for a few seconds while biting my lip, I looked her up and down, smirking.

"Welcome home baby." she greeted me.

"Where's Noah?" I asked, my hands lowering to her waist while she wrapped her hands around my neck.

"He's staying over at my dad's place for a few days. I figured he would want to spend some time with his grandpa, don't you think?" she asked, smirking slightly at me.

"You sure it wasn't just you being too worried about his safety?" I asked, smirking back at her.

"There's nothing wrong with being cautious. Besides, look what I did. We got some time alone together now..." Jane said, batting her eyes seductively at me.

She knew what she did just from what she must have felt on her leg, I was already really hard and I couldn't say she weren't wet just by the sight of me.

"Mmmhm" I hummed, walking forward pushing Jane towards the bed.

"So no kid at home, just the two of us in this large penthouse. I like the sound of that baby. Can I show you how much I like it?" I asked her amusingly.

I didn't need to ask more knowing she wanted me just as bad as I wanted her.

I leaned down again to kiss her but this time it was rough and more passionate than before. The kiss quickly got heated when my hands slid from her face to her side undoing her towel, freeing more of her soft skin for me to touch and mark.

My kiss moved from her lips to her jaw down to her neck, almost immediately finding her sweet spot making her moan out quietly.

Let's just say I make her moan continuously for the rest of the night.

-----

finally another chapter!! sorry i have to end it there, you can figure out what happened next on your own ;)

please VOTE, COMMENT AND FOLLOW!

Chapter 28

WARNING: The following chapter may contain rape/violence content and strong language which may be offensive and/or inappropriate for some readers.

i do NOT tolerate rape or violence in any way! this is only for the sake of this story so please beware!

p.s. pls aware that this chapter is going through very fast but i tried to made it seems as realistic as possible

-----

Jane's POV

I swear something is wrong.

The weather is extremely hot and the scientists are obviously wrong about expecting this year's weather to be cooler.

It was bright and hot outside, the summer air barely cooling off for the day. It was like walking through a sauna, it was a wet heat, the kind that made your hair cling to you the second you stepped outside.

I tried desperately to cover up despite the heat, my dad's cautious words swirling around in my head.

I was washing the dishes by myself, humming away to the melody of the common song that have been played continuously on the radio.

I was just done when I heard some shuffling, and the soft sound of the door creaked. I have no idea who would it be since William is at work and Noah is at my dad's place so I'm all alone in the penthouse today.

I could be wrong but I swear I heard multiple footsteps and voices murmured to each other coming from the living room.

I crept my way to the hallway but I saw nobody. Getting scared, I quickly make my way to the bedroom where my cellphone is also located at.

I was near the bedroom, passing Noah's room when suddenly someone clamped their hand over my mouth and pulled me backward.

"Mhm!" I screamed as their arms closed in a tight grip around me. I struggled to set myself free from the person holding me. I was twisting and wiggling around when this person hissed in my ear, "Stop fighting you stupid bitch!"

It's a voice of a man that I'm not familiar with.

My eyes widened when Sullivan appeared in front of me and helped the person to restrain me.

Before I was even aware of what was happening, they dragged me into my bedroom. My eyes widened and panic rise in me as the door closed from behind us with a bang, and they finally let me go, pushing me to the floor.

Pain flashed in my knees when I hit the ground, and I looked around me in frenzy. I finally noticed that there was only Sullivan and his man in the room.

Their silent, menacing looks froze everything in me and my insides churned with nausea.

No, this can't be happening!

My nightmare has turned into reality!

This is it, the final disaster.

"Sullivan! What are you doing? What's all this?" I asked with a panic in my voice while looking at him and the man beside him. I couldn't believe he would go to this extreme to hurt me or anything.

Sullivan's eyes flashed with hate, his face twisting into an ugly grimace when he took a few steps toward me. I scurried to my feet, backing toward the bed and away from them.

"I warned you woman," Sullivan hissed. "I told you and your stupid fiance to not do anything stupid if he can't handle the risk!" he shouted.

I was breathing so fast now, my whole body paralyzed in terror from the promise of hurt in Sullivan's eyes.

"But he just couldn't listen, can't he?!" He tsked and smiled, a cruel twist to his lips stealing the air out of my lungs. "And now, you'll get to pay for it."

I flinched at his venom words.

Slowly, I pressed my sweaty palms against the bed behind me just as the other guy locked the door, the pounding of my heart becoming louder.

I looked at Sullivan and the guy, their stares were too hostile and both of them looked ready for something much worse than this.

"Don't do this Sullivan. This is wrong and you know William could do worse to you!" I said to Sullivan in a, I hope, threatening way.

He smirked, "Oh pretty girl, I will do this and I will enjoy every second of it. William can go to hell with his fucking lawsuit and shit."

I got a lump in my throat when hearing at his words. Sullivan moved toward me and my fear quickly escalated to horror.

In panic, I dashed toward the door, hoping to be quick enough to elude them and unlock it, but Sullivan's man was faster. He blocked my way and pushed me back.

"Argh! Let me go!" I screamed. I tried to pass the man again but he pushed me and the force of the impact sent me stumble to the floor.

"Foolish girl." Sullivan tsked. "What do you think you're doing huh?"

I looked at Sullivan with my begging eyes. I hated the panic that crept inside of me, making me feel so vulnerable. I tried to think of some solution but there was none. There were two of them, tough and strong, and I was powerless.

The door was locked so no one could come inside. It's not like anyone can hear me from here anyway. They probably didn't know what's happening inside.

I know for a fact that Sullivan is going to hurt me somehow but what I don't know is that how worse it could be.

I was terrified of physical pain and my limbs slowly grew cold because this time there was no way for me to avoid it.

I looked around my room for anything that could help me but there was nothing I could use as a protection. I was trapped without any way to save myself. I really hope to reach for my cellphone on the bedside table but there's no way I could get to it before Sullivan got a grip on me.

I wanted to scream for help even though I know it would be useless because I don't think anyone can hear me but it's worth the try anyway.

"Help-!" I began screaming from the bottom of my lungs as I came back to my feet, desperately hoping for someone to at least hear me but Sullivan moved so quickly that I didn't even manage to finish it before he clamped his hand over my mouth.

I resisted, trying to get away but Sullivan's grip was too strong. I kicked with my legs, managing to make Sullivan lose his balance and stagger, but before I could even set myself free, he pushed me to my knees forcefully and tightened his grip on me. Sullivan's hand preventing me from screaming and I realized that there's nothing I could do.

"Stop resisting you slut!" Sullivan said harshly.

His eyes were filled with hatred and disgust. Dread clutched onto me. My tears had already pooled in my eyes, blurring my vision.

"You deserve the worst bitch. This is what you get when you and your fucking man tryna mess with me." Sullivan said while grabbing my hair, raising it in the air.

I broke out in cold sweat as I listened to his words. My heart was about to burst, but not in the school girl crush type of way. This is the I'm gonna die soon type of way.

"You're such a tease you know." Sullivan whispered in my ear. "Now, let's see if you can handle me teasing you." He said while smirking.

I gasped. "Please don't. Please."

Sullivan hungrily whispered into my ear, "You don't have a choice pretty girl."

I began to struggle against him, trashing trying to get out of his strong hold. It was no use though, I wasn't a ninja, and I surely couldn't over power him. He towered over me by at least a good head and his frame was slightly bigger than my petite one.

"Sullivan... please stop..." I pleaded.

He kissed my mouth to silence me. I was in a slight panic and could focus on nothing but the man thinking about rapping me.

"Get out and make sure no one's here." Sullivan said but not addressing anyone. I know it was meant for the guy as I saw him nodded while smirking slightly at me and walked out of the room, leaving me alone with Sullivan.

I started to struggle again, trying to shove Sullivan away from me long enough to run away and hide till I was out of this stage. But nothing I did worked.

Sullivan was quick to pushed me on the bed and hovered over me. His hand that wasn't holding my hands above my head was sailing around my body looking for treasure, his first stop is my breast. He began needing them tenderly causing me to let out an unpleasant moan into his mouth as he was kissing me.

He rasped, "Do you not want this?" His kiss trailed down to my jaw, then my throat. His hand that had been on my breast trailed down, down, under my shirt, through my bra, and he flicked a nipple.

I whimpered quietly and prayed that someone would hear and help me.

Sullivan's hand pulled the bra down and that said hand began cupping my breast. Moving and touching. My eyes rolled back and I fisted my hands and bit my lip hard to stop my body from vibrating.

Sullivan growled, "I wanna taste you." He nipped at my skin more. "You must taste so good. So sweet... mmm."

I squirmed, trying to break free from his hard grip on me. "I-Uh-P-Please! Let me go! If money is what you want then take it, take all of it I don't care! Just please... don't hurt me. Don't do this Sullivan." I begged him.

This was not happening! I could not let him rape me!

He soon became frustrated with my shirt and pulled it over me and threw it on the ground somewhere. I cried and shook my head, tried to get my hands lose to cover myself. When that didn't work, I tried turning my body so I wasn't facing him. That didn't work either. I tried to struggle again.

I let out a very faint sigh and accidently arched my back causing my chest to be pushed closer to Sullivan. He chuckled.

"Sounds to me you want me to do this huh?"

I quickly shook my head. "N-no! Pl-please stop!"

Sullivan tsked, "I'm afraid I can't..."

My eyes began to swell with tears as I felt his hand slid down from my breast to my stomach and downward till he was in my pants, cupping my sex with his hand applying pressure.

I cried in need but he ignored me.

Sullivan whispered, "I can't take it anymore. Your scent is driving me insane." His voice was horse from lust.

My stomach turned into a mash of horror and repugnance. Each part of me screamed in protest, my breathing becoming erratic and several beads of sweat formed on my temples.

He is going to force me. This is rape! My heart pounded against my rib cage and I tried to inhale deeply.

My wide eyes followed him as he unfasten his belt. I stared at him in schock and aversion. He watched me with amusement as he went for the top button of his jeans, holding me in place with his other hand on my shoulder.

I trashed around, the disgust and fear of what was about to happen drowning me.

I heard a zipper and my eyes widened as he pulled out his dick. I was feeling madly disgusted and tried to hold back my tears.

I began to struggle again. "Sullivan no! Don't! I'm begging you! Please don't!" I screamed loudly. I trembled as tears ran down my face.

"Quiet!" He said, slapping me. It made me wince and erupt in new tears.

"Stop! Stop this please!" I shouted with tears on my face.

Sullivan raised his hand and slapped me again. It hurt and sting so much. "Shut up you whore!" He shouted back.

"Get off me! You are a sick bastard! No wonder everyone hates you and your life is miserable because you deserves it!" I shouted angrily at him.

I hunched when Sullivan raised his hand, expecting him to hit me again, but he grabbed my chin and made me look at him. "After I finish playing with you, I'm going to torture you and make you feel as miserable as my life. Now keep quiet!"

I can't let him do that. I need to be strong. Thinking about Noah and William motivates me to do something and defend myself rather than surrender to the devil.

So I began struggling, twisting and moving my whole body as fear guided me. "Go to hell! Let me go, you bastard!" I screamed, burning from exertion and pain, and fought even harder.

Sullivan pulled my hair harshly. "If I tell you to keep quiet, you will keep quiet you bitch!"

"No! You are a son of a bitch! A freaking psychopath." I hissed.

Before Sullivan could move further, I bared my teeth and bit his forearm. I quickly jump to my feet again when he drew back with a hiss.

"You're sick!" I screamed and ran away from him as fast as I could, heading out to the living room, but I could barely cross several feet before Sullivan caught me and pushed me to the floor. I fell with a thud, but then he grabbed me by my hair and yanked it, hitting my head against the hard surface.

"Argh! Stop!" I screamed, horrified to be abused by him like this.

Sullivan didn't stop as he came above me, landing his fist on my rib cage that forced the bile up my throat. I was screaming and trashed against him. He did it so mercilessly until I was a broken mess on the floor, unable to move from an enormous amount of pain.

"You're crazy if you think you could run away from me!" The truth is, he looked crazy, his face viciously twisted as he dragged me by hair over the floor to the bed. My scream of pain came out ragged, interrupted by my heavy breathing. Sullivan pushed me up to the bed, my limp body laying lifelessly on it.

"Looks like your life is in miserable right now. Well no shit, you deserves it bitch." Sullivan hissed, using my own words against me.

I was crying silently and praying hard that Noah and William are alright. If this is what it takes for me to safe my son and the love of my life from harm and pain, then so be it.

-----

surprise surprise! new chapter again! i feel so bad for constantly leaving you guys with slow updates :(

i don't know how to feel about this chapter and i was honestly scared to post it because i never experience anything close to rape and it could be offensive so if anyone out there ever went through that i just hope you're ok and you deserves all the happiness in the world for your bravery <3

please VOTE, COMMENT AND FOLLOW!

Chapter 29

Jane's POV

My head hurts so much and the room spins like a nightmare version of merry-go-round that I can't escape.

I can't see clearly but I know for sure that the figure above me right now is Sullivan. I try to push him away but my whole body aches and feel heavy.

The hit from Sullivan makes me black out for a couple of seconds. I heard someone shouted from far and also the sound of slamming doors. The last thing I heard was Sullivan muttered a "Shit" before my eyes were closed.

When I gain my conscious back, I saw a body was laying on the ground. I heard a grunt from another figure and the sound of their footsteps echoing in the room as he walk slowly towards me.

I got up to run, this sudden stranger seemed to be stronger than both Sullivan and his man combined. My eyes were still a bit blurry so I can't see the figure clearly.

I had just gotten to my feet when the man's hand wrapped around me and I was pulled into his chest.

Getting scared again, I scream while hitting whatever part of him that I could.

"Shh shh... Jane, it's okay. Baby, it's me. It's me, William." He said softly while stroking my hair.

I looked up, making sure it was really him before my legs gave out. William quickly caught me, helping me sit down on the bed and once again he wrapped his arms around me.

My whole body was shaking when I said, "William, I'm sorry. I should have told to you, I-I should... I-I'm sorry. I didn't know he S-Sullivan he was g-going to h-hurt me." I gushed, unable to stop the flow of heavy tears I was now shedding as William cradled me in his arms.

"Darling, you didn't know this was going to happen. You didn't know okay? Don't take it out on yourself. You're safe now baby. You're safe with me." William soothed, kissing my forehead.

Although I was still shaken up, I couldn't help but thank any supernatural being I could think of for delivering William Winston to me. He was not only my fiance but my hero as well. As I sat there crying in his arms, I couldn't help but think about how grateful I am to always have him by my side.

"Will?"

"Yes darling?" He asked.

"I love you" I murmured, burying my head into his chest.

William chuckled, "I love you too Jane. But as much as I like to cuddle with you right now, I have other much important things to do."

"What?" I questioned him.

"Baby, I can't let Sullivan's unconscious body laying forever on our bedroom floor. It's not really the kind of sight I would like to see you know?" William joked, smile amusingly.

I slap William's chest slightly at his attempt for making a joke in this situation.

He laughed, "Okay okay I'm sorry. But really though. I gotta call the cops. Then we need to go to the hospital to see if you were injured."

I nodded at him. "I think my bones are broken."

"Shit, does it hurt? I'm sorry baby. I should have come sooner. What did that bastard do to you?" William asked out of concerned.

I winced a little remembering what had happened. "Can't remember. I guess he punched me twice. And almost raped me."

"Baby... god I wish I could just kill him right now." William said while looking at Sullivan's currently unconscious body with distaste and anger.

We heard noises from the living room. I clutched tightly on William, scared of who would it be.

"It's okay baby. I guess that was the cops. I've told the security earlier to call them." William explained.

My breathing went normal again as I nodded at his words.

My gaze fell on the digital clock on the bedside table. Suddenly, I realized that it was only 3pm and it was way too early for William to be home from work. "William? Why are you home so early? How did you know Sullivan was here?" I asked curiously.

"About that huh. Actually I got a call from Sullivan this morning. Few days ago after he threatened you, I sued him and sent a lawsuit against him. Don't blame me, I was mad he had the nerves to go and see you. So yeah he went crazy during the phone call." William shrugged, "Then later, Fred called me and said he found Sullivan's car just around here but he didn't saw him getting into the house. But of course Sullivan would be here because he wanted to get back at me for what I did to him so I told Fred to look for you and call the cops while I made my way here as soon as I can."

"You didn't tell me you sent him a lawsuit! And uh who's Fred?" I asked sheepishly.

William smile nervously. "I forgot to tell you. Fred is kind of your bodyguard. He was supposed to be guarding the penthouse and look out for you and Noah when I'm not home. But from what happened today, I'm not sure if he can still keep his job. He sure is a careless guy and we don't need people like him-"

"I didn't know you got me a bodyguard." I laughed. "It reminds me of those rich people who always have their bodyguards following them around. I don't think it's necessary but thank you." I smile sweetly at William.

"Anything for you. I guess we could give Fred another chance. After all, he's still new." William chuckled.

I let out a small laugh, "Sure babe."

The day goes on with William settling with the cops. Sullivan was taken to the hospital while the cops still have their eyes on him. Later, he will be taken to the court to sort out his penance by the law.

While William was busy with Sullivan's case, I was getting checked at the hospital.

After checking in, I was referred to a triage nurse who is trained to assess the severity of my condition. The triage nurse did a brief exam and checked my vital signs, such as temperature and blood pressure. I was lucky that I'm not seriously ill and injured. The diagnostic tests and minor first-aid procedures, such as applying ice packs and cleaning my wounds also have been done by the nurse.

An hour later I was done getting checked the same time William arrived at the hospital. Unfortunately, I was admitted to the hospital but the doctor said it won't be long. If my wounds seem to heal faster they probably let me go home by tomorrow.

I was lying in the hospital bed while William was pacing back and forth before sitting nervously while watching my heart monitor.

I studied my room slowly. Low light on at all times, and there are cords hanging down for the nurses call button and the IV solutions.

There is also an electronic machine sitting on a cart with odd wires leading from it and a privacy curtain hanging from a track on the ceiling.

There is no get well soon card on the bedside table. Only a bouquet of fresh flowers that William managed to buy for me while he was on his way to the hospital earlier.

I squirmed a little in the hospital bed, searching for the comfort of my own bed at home. At least I was lucky that I don't have IV's in my arms, a breathing tube or an oxygen mask. I only have a few bandages on my limbs and visible stitches that makes me cringe whenever I look at it.

"Baby, you alright?" William asked me.

I nodded, "Yeah, just missing home. I don't think it's necessary for me to be admitted in the hospital. We can just hire a doctor to look after me at home right?"

William chuckled, "I know you don't like hospital babe but they can give you a better treatment in here. It's fine, if you don't like it here then I'll ask the doctor if you could check out tomorrow."

"Thank you." I smiled adoringly at him.

"Like I said, anything for you." William stood up and kissed me on the forehead.

"Hey, did you call my dad?" I asked.

William shook his head, "No I didn't. I'm not sure if I should tell him right away."

I sighed. "You're right. William can you please don't tell my dad about this? It's better if we keep this as a secret." I told William.

"Jane, I thought there will be no more secrets between you and your dad. I know he will get worry but don't you think he deserves to know about this? About what happened to you?"

I frowned and sighed for the second time. "Okay. We'll tell him. But can we wait until I check out from the hospital? I don't think now is the right time."

Upon seeing my tears and my immense pain, William cradled me in his arms like I would do to a new born baby. I felt all warm and loved and not in the least bit frighten.

"I will make sure Sullivan will get what he deserves for what he had done to you baby. I'm sorry you have to go through that pain. I love you Jane. I love you so much." William whispered in my ear.

I gave him a small, fragile smile as I whispered haltingly, "...sorry... William."

Tears welling up in his eyes as he shook his head in disbelief. "No Jane. I'm the one that's sorry for leaving you alone. I should have been there by your side to protect you darling."

His eyes were full of worry. Was that remorse I also saw there? I reached up and cradled his jaw for a moment, while I focused on his face and whispered, "You aren't angry at me?"

William shifted on the hospital bed and searched my face as if he was memorizing it. Then he shook his head sadly and slowly. Bending over me, his lips met mine. At first he was very gentle but then he kissed me with more urgency while continuing to fill me with his life force through his breath.

The comfort we gave each other at that moment was one full of thankfulness. He was glad I was alive and I was glad for his ability to save me.

Ending the kiss, he focused on me and whispered, "Oh Jane, I thought I was going to lose you." I can feel the fear and misery coloring each of his words.

I sobbed into his chest, "I know. I'm sorry William. I love you and I'm sorry."

William kissed my head. "Shh, I love you too. I love you so much." Then he kissed my eyebrow, "You and I, always." And lastly he kissed my lips, "I am so lucky to have such a beautiful and strong lady by my side."

I smiled and looked at William in the eyes as I shook my head playfully and said, "Careful Mr. CEO, your soft side is showing."

William laughed heartily, "Only for you Jane. Only for you." He smiled adoringly at me, "And our child."

By child, I know he meant Noah. But I can't help wondering how would it be to have William's rightful child. Maybe in the future.

Only time will tell.

!

Chapter 30

Jane's POV

A day has passed and I am currently sitting on the hospital bed, waiting for William while he is paying for my hospital bill.

I have changed the blue hospital gown to my own casual wear consist of black jeans and a caramel T-shirt. It feels good to finally get to wear my own clothes.

I stretch my muscles a little and heard my bones cracked and pop. There's something about cracking my back that I found so unbelievably satisfying. It's a good thing because I once read in a health magazine that stretching exercises can help relieve pain and tension in the back.

My body still ached a little here and there but I think I'm strong enough to walk on my own now even though the wounds and bruises on my body haven't completely heal yet.

I heard his footsteps before he opened the door to my hospital room. William finally came into view, matching a perfect white button up shirt with a neat pair of jeans and a stylish pair of boots. Only William can make a plain white shirt look sexy while he's wearing it. However, he once said that it takes no style to make a white shirt look good, as long as it is clean and it fits.

I am pretty much convince that I look like a potato next to him.

William walked over to me. He smiles and lean closer to kiss me but accidentally pressed his hand on my legs, making me whine.

"Oh my god babe! I'm sorry, did it hurt?" William asked in concerned while carefully examining me.

"It's fine, nothing hurts." I lied and smiled at him but he just keep looking at me. William's pained expression intensified and I felt a pang of guilt in my chest.

"Baby are you sure you're okay?" William asked and I can't look at him in the eye. I don't want to ruin this day. The day's just starting and I finally about to discharge from the hospital. We're going to pick up Noah later, since we haven't been with him for some time so we want to make every moment today with Noah as splendid as possible.

"Hey, we have to go and get Noah today." I said and looked at William while smiling. I know that my smile could always calm him down and I am always right.

His expression softens as soon as he sees me smile and that made me feel better somehow.

William staring admiringly at my face and I smiled at him. "Yeah I miss him. Can't wait to see the little guy soon." he said.

William just finished preparing the car so he went to get my bags and I tried to stand up but he turned to me and spoke, "No, wait. Let me."

"What?" I said disbelievingly.

William positioned his hands on my lower back and under my legs.

"Wait! What are you doing Will—"

"It's fine. I'll carry you babe." William told me.

"Oh god, seriously William? No! What would people say—"

He turned to look at me once again and said, "Jane, I don't want to see you struggling to walk so I'll carry you. Just let me carry you to the car please."

I did as what he said and I felt my eyes moist. He'd certainly do everything just to see me feel comfortable.

"We can just ask for a wheelchair you know. It'll be much easier." I giggled.

William only smirk at me,"Now babe, why would you need a wheelchair when you have me to carry you to the edge of the world?"

I smile adoringly at William. I'm in love with an angel and I'm so lucky to have him.

-

When we arrived at my dad's house, Noah was quick to run and hug me tightly. I know I should give him time to get used to our return, but I just can't contain myself. I missed my baby so much.

I grab him up, coo and kiss him. I don't care how affectionate I'm being at the moment, he's my son after all.

"Aw my baby!" I croon. "Did you miss me? Did you miss mommy?"

"Mommy! I've been waiting for you. I miss you and daddy everyday!" Noah exclaimed. He takes it well, considering.

"Hey, daddy want some hugs too!" I heard William shouted from behind me which makes both Noah and I laugh.

After picking up Noah at my dad's house, we spent half an hour talking with my dad about what happened. Let just say he didn't seem so happy about it. My dad keeps talking about how careless William has been in taking care of me, and how I was too stubborn to stay longer at the hospital where I should be getting a proper treatment. After a while, my dad went from being angry to feeling terrifically upset.

Finally, we exchanged goodbyes with my dad and made our way to the nearest beach.

I was thinking we could go to any of the nearest theme park or shopping mall but William decided to go for a picnic by the beach. Apparently, William exclaimed that it will be much more relaxing, especially for me since I just got out from the hospital and still haven't fully recovered yet.

I didn't really mind where we would be spending our day, and picnic actually did sound like a great idea, considering that Noah is also up for the spontaneous family picnic.

Our unplanned picnic allow us to eat, play and spend quality time together which we haven't gotten to do enough lately.

William stopped at the nearby grocery store to buy some foods, drinks, and snacks for us. He also managed to grab a basket, plates, cups, and a plaid blue blanket.

Our picnic menus include tuna salad, veggies, sandwiches and some fresh fruits that would make a healthy snack. We even pick up a pepperoni pizza on our way to the beach.

Once we arrived, I couldn't seem to stop gawking at the stunning view of the beautiful beach. It is probably because of the whiteness of the sand and the clarity of the water. My mind relaxed at the sound of the waves while feeling the sand between my toes.

Later, I found myself alone on the blanket, eating some blackcurrants with an orange citrus drink. Meanwhile, William and Noah are playing by the water.

William has changed his expensive boots to a much comfortable Nike's flip flop. He even rolled his pants up to his thighs to avoid it from getting drenched by the beach water.

I can never get tired of watching my fiance having his time playing around with our son. It was indeed every women's favorite sight.

We took a walk on the beach just before sunset. We could not help admiring the beautiful sunset. Noah exclaimed the view was gorgeous. I asked him where did he learned the word and he told us about my dad's story regarding his wife, which is my mom, was a really gorgeous lady. Noah said that the word means beautiful when he once asked grandpa, and he thought the view on the sunset on the beach was beautiful too so he pointed out that it was gorgeous.

It was gorgeous, indeed.

Our walks come to a halt halfway on the shoreline when Noah suddenly stopped in front of us.

"Mommy, I think you are more gorgeous than the sunset." Noah said while looking up at me. In seconds, I lift him up, hug him, kiss the little pink heart of his nose.

"I love you so much sweetheart. And I think you're gorgeous too." I giggled and Noah joined me. William put his arms around me so we could have a family hug.

Smiling happily and feeling content, William whispered loud enough for the three of us to hear, "You two are incredibly gorgeous and I have no idea what have I done to deserves you two in my life. I love you both so much. My little family. My beloved."

A smile lights up my face, thanking whoever is up above who kept an eye on me, making William cross my path in a trivial circumstances.

After a few more minutes watching the sunset, we cleaned up and packed our things in the basket and went home. Noah fell asleep in the car while on our way home from the beach.

Once we arrived at the penthouse, William carry a sleepy Noah in his arm while carrying the picnic basket and both Noah's and my duffel bag inside. He ignored my pleas to help carry the bags, or at least just the basket.

He told me that I was lucky Noah was with us or else he would already have carried me all the way from the car to our bedroom. I only smiled and shrugged my shoulder while following him inside.

I followed William to Noah's bedroom. Noah started to squirm a bit so William sing softly in his ear as he started to drift off in a graceful sleep again. We both took turns to kiss Noah before we went to our bedroom.

"Well done Mr. Winston." I whispered to William.

William turned to me and a smirk slowly making its way to his face.

These last couple of months with William have been amazing, despite what happened with Sullivan, and I don't think I could ever love anyone as much as I love William.

I was already seated on our bed, when I suddenly felt his hand on my leg. I look over at him and smile.

"What are you thinking about baby?" He asked, grabbing my hand.

"You, and how much my life has changed these past couple of months. You've made me and Noah happier than we've been in a long time. William, thank you for loving me unconditionally." I whispered, tears brimming in my eyes. William raises his hand and wipes it.

"You don't have to thank me baby. If anything, I should be thanking you for making me the happiest man alive." William told me.

I smile at him and lean over to kiss his cheek. William cupped my face in his hands and smile at me. I put my hand against his chest and pushed him back onto the bed and giggling while getting on top of him.

I blushed softly as my heart raced. I kissed him softly at first and smiled as I made it more passionate. His heart beat hard against my palms as he kissed me back, wrapping his arms around my waist. I blushed again as my heart raced almost in time with his.

William broke the kiss, then moved down to kiss my neck and trailed his hands up my back.

I blushed heavily and looked in his eyes, he looked back into mine and not saying a word.

I didn't know how I could turn him on like they do in the romance movies. I kissed his neck lightly and a soft moan left his throat, almost like a low growl.

I smiled, "Shh, we don't want little Noah to think that there's a big bad wolf trying to eat his mommy."

William chuckled, looking at me, "But it is true, isn't it? This big bad wolf wants to have a taste of his mommy. Let's see if the mommy can hold her scream."

I took a sharp breath in as William trailed his hands across my arms. I rolled over so William was on top of me and I pulled his white shirt off of him. I felt his heart jumped as I traced his chest.

"Are you sure you wanna go on?" William asked. "I don't want to hurt you baby. You haven't completely heal yet."

I thought for a moment before nodding my head. "It's okay. I can manage. Please Will..."

William had his arms next to my head to lift him up so he wouldn't crash me. He lowered his head and kissed me again. My back arched up to him, pressing my body against his and I kissed him back passionately.

He moaned deeply, lowering his body and pressing my body against the bed. I smiled and continued to kiss him.

"God, Jane, your body is perfect and I need you-" He was stopped in mid thought as the heat from my body began to drive him crazy.

I rolled over again so I could straddle him. I pulled his jeans along with his boxer. My underwear also came off and I mounted him again. As I sat there on him, I bent down to whisper in his ear.

"You ready?" I asked and he nodded his head eagerly.

Seconds later, I can see William in a state of suspense. I squeeze tight where he was unable to thrust or pull out. At the same time he asked me, "Wait, shouldn't I put on the protection?"

"Yeah, but it's okay if you don't want to. I mean, we could try... right?" I blurted out.

"Y-yeah. We can try, oh god that's good. Yeah baby, let's see if we can get Noah a little brother." William said with a strangled moan.

I nodded, "Or a little sister."

William chuckled at me, "Sure babe."

The feeling makes me hot and wild, I was sweating a little but I didn't mind one bit as William's warmth felt wonderful on me. His gentleness makes my heart melt.

He licked my nipples and neck, then blowing on the marks he had left on my body. He also kissed all the bruises on my body that are slowly healing with his warm and gentle kisses. The night went off as William left more sensual kisses around my chest.

Epilogue

Jane's POV

7 years later

The television was playing an old popular romance movie. I've been spending too much time watching movies during weekend. This is probably because I don't have much time during weekdays since I've been working myself out until late night.

3 years ago, after I graduated my bachelor degree online, I just poked around a little thinking I'd send out a few resumes and have a job by the end of the month. Fast forward 2 months later, with a little help from William, I have finally gotten myself a job as a HR specialist in Chase & Co. Inc.

No surprised there when William insisted for me to stay home and look pretty. Meanwhile, I would rather make myself work to not let my degree go to waste.

When the movie didn't excite me anymore, I paused to admire my outrageously expensive and very sparkly wedding ring on my left hand. I still couldn't believe that William and I have officially, legally married.

How long has it been? 6 and a half year I supposed? That was long enough.

Our wedding was not as massive as people would have thought. I asked William to make it simple but elegant. And he managed to do just that.

I heard the familiar sound of the front door opening, then closing, and assumed William and the kids are back. The loud voices of excitement from my kids can be heard from the living room.

I saw my little 7 year old girl first, as she was running happily towards me with her brother followed behind.

"Mommy! We're back!" Ellie shouted. She ran and hugged me tightly. Her hair was up in a cute pigtails that I did for her this morning.

It's Saturday and Ellie woke up this morning asking for chocolate milk and donuts which we were unfornately lack of it. William who was already wrapped around her little finger, cannot resist the cute little pout and round eyes of Ellie. So he decided to bring the kids, Noah and Ellie, to the nearest cafe and bought some sparkly donuts for all of us.

Maybe it was that cute little toothless smile, or the dimples on Ellie's cheeks. I didn't know exactly what it was, but all it took was some puppy eyes and a little pout to make William cave.

Ellie hadn't even learned how to make her own bed but she was a manipulative mastermind when she set her mind on something, and I had to admit I was kind of proud of her for that. She'd be a powerful, beautiful woman one day.

"Hey sweetie, what did you buy?" I asked Ellie while picking her up to sit on my lap. Noah also come running in and sit besides me on the couch.

"We buy donuts, mommy! Lots of donuts! Daddy said we can have donuts for dinner too." Ellie exclaimed happily.

I glared my eyes playfully, "Really? Daddy told you that? Because I don't think we'll be having donuts for dinner. I'll cook something special for us tonight honey."

"Mom, daddy bought lots of donuts. He bought 2 full boxes of it!" Noah told me.

I laughed, knowing William too well that he'll buy anything the kids want.

"Your daddy literally has a soft spot for you two." I said, smiling.

"Only for my family." I heard William's voice said. I looked up to see my handsome husband, with 2 boxes of donuts in one hand while the other looks like he held 2 cartons of chocolate milk.

William put the milks and donuts on the table and was quick to join us on the couch. He sit besides Noah which make the little guy being sandwiched between William and me. Poor boy, but he didn't seem to mind getting the affection he deserves from his parents.

"We are not having donuts for dinner, William." I told him while he mindlessly reaching for the remote to change the channel on the tv.

William only hummed, "Why not babe?"

I sighed, "Hun, I've told you too much sugar is not good for the kids. Sugar can make them hyper."

William laughed, "It's only once in a blue moon babe. Give the kids some fun."

I sighed, "Nuh uh, I'm making butter crusted shrimp pasta with broccoli."

"Mom no!" Noah whined.

"Ew broccoli!" Ellie cry.

William laughed again at the kids' reaction as I shrugged my shoulders, "What? Why? My pasta taste just fine, alright. And broccoli is good for your growth so stop complaining."

"Nuh uh. Broccoli no." Ellie stated, may I say sternly.

"I swear Ellie is 99% look after you." William said, smile adoringly at Ellie who is currently pouting. "She's hard headed just like you."

I fake shocked, "Excuse me? I'm not hard headed. If anything you are hard headed Mr. ceo."

"Only when I'm working, but never with my family." William points out.

"Mommy, daddy, can we eat the donuts now?" Ellie asked.

I nodded my head and kissed the crown of her head, "Sure sweetie, but don't eat too much. Keep the rest for tomorrow."

"Yay donuts!" Ellie exclaimed, getting off of my lap and ran to get to her donuts. Apparently, Ellie has a thing for donuts while Noah is more into chicken nuggets. I shake my head at the thought, my kids are definitely something different.

"Noah, why don't you go and help your little sister with the donuts while I have a serious talk with your mother on how to get rid of the broccoli for tonight's dinner." William told Noah with a sly smile.

"Okay. Good luck dad!" Noah laughed and went with Ellie to bring the donuts into the kitchen. Even for a 10 year old, Noah can be very helpful at watching over his little sister when I'm busy. Though sometimes the kids can be pretty handful too.

"So about the broccoli..." William started.

I giggled, "Are you seriously want to consider about getting rid of the broccoli? God, you're something else Will."

"But babe," He whined, "Let the kids have what they want sometimes. Besides, it's Saturday. They deserves to have donuts for dinner on a Saturday night."

I laughed, "Who made that up? I'm their mother. I only do what's best for my kids. Now, I don't wanna argue about this."

"We're not arguing. This is discussing babe." William stated.

"Sure. But still, no donuts for dinner. You're spoiling them too much." I said.

"Mhmm, they're my kids. I only do what's best for my kids." He mocked me by copying my words from earlier.

"Stop. I'm gonna prepare for dinner now." I told him as I stood up ready to go to the kitchen. But I didn't get to go far when William's hand reached for mine, stopping me.

"Let's have some time together while the kids are busy with their donuts." William said, smirking.

I gasped, "Oh my, William, please don't tell me you bought the donuts to distract them so you could get laid?"

"What? No, of course not. But since they were distracted at the moment, let's make the most if it. We gotta appreciate every moment babe." William said slyly as he stood up as well.

William was about to kiss me when suddenly Ellie come running in, "Mommy! Daddy!"

I was quick to put a distance between William and me. My little daughter really didn't need to see the pda from her parents right now.

"Honey, what's wrong? Have you ate your donuts?" I asked her while I smoothen her hair.

"Yes, my donuts are pretty! They have sprinkles all over it mommy! I love it!" Ellie told us.

William pick her up and kiss her head tenderly. "That's good sweetie. I'll buy more donuts for you next time. Now, why don't you go with your brother before he finishes all your pretty donuts. Mommy and daddy got something to do. We'll join both of you later, alright?"

"Alright daddy!" Ellie replied and quickly ran back to the kitchen.

I instantly looked at William. "What was that for? We got nothing to do together, I gotta prepare the dinner William."

William quickly reached for my waist and dragged me to our bedroom.

"It's been a while since we got time together Mrs. Winston. Let me have you all for myself right now." William whispered seductively into my ear.

"William I'm serious. If you behave right now, you might just get what you wanted tonight. So let me go and prepare our dinner in peace, you'll get the reward later." I told him.

"Mmm, what kind of reward baby? 5 blowjobs?" He asked, smirking.

I giggled. "That's too much so no. But I may ride you on our bed tonight. And I would go on as long as you want me to." I told him, my voice came out almost like a whisper.

"Okay. I like the sound of that. Now go and make your famous pasta. Don't keep me waiting darling." William let me go and slap my ass as I walk my way to the kitchen where the kids are.

"Behave, big guy." I said slowly to William with a wink before entering the kitchen.

While I was preparing the dinner, William put on a disney movie to watch with the kids. He even poured some chocolate milk for them to drink during the movie.

After I was done cooking, we all took our seats on the dining table to eat. Ellie and Noah both had their shrimp and pasta with only one broccoli each.

I was too tired to even argue with them on how they are supposed to eat more veggies. I guess next time.

When we all finished with our dinner, I went to wash the dishes while William offered to help the kids to take their bath. After I was done cleaning, I went to join William putting the kids into bed.

Ellie has already fell asleep as I kissed her head and wish her good night. Next, I entered Noah's room and I saw William was helping Noah getting ready for bed.

"Sweet dreams big guy. Daddy loves you so much."

Noah smiled. "I love you too daddy. And uh daddy, can we play soccer tomorrow?"

"Sure buddy, but you gotta sleep first. Good night." William replied and kissed his head.

"Good night daddy." Noah replied sleepily.

My heart grows at the sight. I'm still grateful for William to love Noah just like his own son. I couldn't ask for anything better than this. I'm so happy and thankful for my little family.

"Hello little man." I smiled.

"Hi mommy, I'm about to sleep now." Noah told me.

"Okay sweetie. Have a good night. Mommy loves you." I told him and kissed his cheek.

After that, I turn off the lights to Noah's room and went to my bedroom with William by my side.

"I love seeing you with the kids." I beamed as I changed into an oversized shirt and only underwear, "You're so good with them."

William chuckled as he did the same, except he changed into only a sweatpants. "I guess you're right. I've always been so natural with children."

I snaked my hands around his waist and rest my lips on his broad shoulder. "See?" I whispered into his skin, "All this parenting doesn't seem so bad now, does it?"

"Yeah, you're right. I love our family so much. I can't wait to have more kids with you." said William, smiling at the thought of having more kids that will look a little bit like him and a little bit like me.

I chuckled, "Okay, maybe in the future mister. You only want them so you'll have an army of pretty kids to admire you."

"Not true Jane. Honestly, I love being a dad. As long as you're the mother." William said truthfully.

"Of course you do. You're a great dad. Sometimes I think the kids love you more than me." I sighed.

"Again, not true." William said as he walked towards me. He slowly kissed my cheek before pulling my oversized top off of me.

"William..." I sighed again.

"What babe? After all, you did promised to ride me on our bed tonight. I'm being a good dad aren't I?" William whispered into my ear.

"Darling, you are so beautiful, I can't even put it into words. You astound me with your beauty everyday. You entice and entrap me. You baffle me. You're such an amazing mother to our kids. You're such a perfect wife to me. Why don't you see this? Why can't you see just how lovely you really are? I love you. I fell in love with everything about you. I simply just want you always and forever." William confessed.

How could I be mad at him? After that confession? He's my husband, the love of my life. Ever. I let my gaze fall on him. My eyes filled with tears left to be unshed and his with the upmost sincerity.

I reached out and put my hand on his cheek then stood on my tippy toes and kissed him.

The urgency I felt was shown through the kiss. William backed me to the bed, mouths still attached. I fell back and moved up to give him some room. He climbed up between my legs, placing mine outside of his. He gazed at me with such admiration that I thought my heart was going to explode.

William's hands ran from my shoulders down to my arms. His hands stopped at my hips and started rubbing small circles. I let my teeth graze over his lip and pulled it, biting his lip in the process. William growled and grabbed onto my ass. His long fingers digging into my flesh, leaving his mark on me.

William looked into my eyes with such longing and passion that I couldn't even begin to comprehend what I was feeling. His lips touched mine with a feather like feeling, small little kisses. This was what I needed. Wanted. Craved for. This was my William, the man I fell in love with.

"Thought I'm supposed to be on top tonight?" I whispered questioningly.

"That's okay baby. Let me take care of you tonight. Also I don't think I can last long if you ride me." I smiled at him.

He smiled back and placed himself at my entrance. I widened my legs to give him some more space. He pushed into me and I gasped. It had been around a month since we actually had some time being intimate.

"Ugh. You feel so good. Even better." said William.

I could feel him stretching me out. William's head dipped to the crook of my neck and he growled. He brought his hips back and pushed into me again and again. Slow, steady, deep.

I moaned at the feeling. "C'mon Will. Yes, faster."

William reached up to the headboard behind me, placing one hand on it and the other hand pushing my hips into the bed. He built up the pace, rocking into me. He was going faster now but just as deep. William let go of one of my hip and reached down to place my leg on his shoulder. He placed his hand back on my hip and started pounding into me. Hips against hips, mouth against mouth.

The headboard was now bashing against the wall, leaving dents in it. That's how hard and fast he was giving it to me. I felt my release on the brink when William moaned into my mouth.

"Let go for me baby." William whispered in a raspy voice. I released around him, saying his name over and over again.

A few seconds and deep thrusts later, William found his release. Yelling my name and professing his love for me. "Oh fuc-! Jane, baby. I love you!"

"That's it Will. I love you more." I told him encouragingly.

William collapsed on top of me and rolled off me, pulling me to him before cradling me in his arms. He pressed a soft kiss to my temple and sighed in content.

An hour or two later, William and I were still lying in bed but now tangled up in the covers. We were lucky that we didn't wake up the kids with our hot little session.

"How did we end up here? How did I get so lucky to have the three of you in my life?" I asked William in a low whisper.

William shrugged, "I questioned myself the same thing everyday."

I smiled against his chest. William sighed, a huge grin spreading over his face. Gently, he leaned forward and pressed a kiss to my cheek, whispering in my ear, "I have a gorgeous wife, two beautiful kids, more than enough money and a nice job. I am now convinced that my life is beyond perfect."

I chuckled, "Same goes with me, Mr. ceo."

The End

Bonus Chapter

Jane's POV

I have fond memories of watching cartoons all day long. I can clearly remember the morning Nickelodeon debuted and I spent every Saturday morning firmly planted in front of the screen watching my favorite shows. I may not remember the names of all the state capitols, but I can still sing the theme from Hey Arnold!.

But right now seeing my two kids were captivated by the modern day cartoon playing on the TV makes me worried. Just now I realized that I have been letting Noah and Ellie spent too much time watching TV and playing iPad.

Looking out from the balcony I saw the sun filtered through the clouds, signaling the end of the rain. A golden glow spread across the sky as the sun chased the dark clouds. I was supposed to go out today with my office mates, we plan to have a little break after a tough week at the office. Unfortunately, William and I have decided that weekends are for family. It is the only time we get to spend the day together since we all will be busy during weekdays; me and William have to work while Ellie and Noah goes to school.

"Babe, it's okay. Really, you should go. You need it after working so hard." William told me for the tenth time.

I sighed and frowning slightly. I was worried to leave William alone with the kids since I know how handful those two kids could be but William has assured me that they will be fine.

"I don't know Will, they can be pretty hard to handle sometimes. Are you sure you can handle them alone?" I asked William while looking at Ellie and Noah who are still watching their favorite show on TV.

William looked at me bewildered. "Really Jane? Don't you have a little faith at me? They are my kids, of course I know how to look for them. Now go, your friends must have been waiting for you long enough. If you bail on them they probably think you're such a boring person."

I gasped at him. "Hey! I am not boring. I know how to have fun. I'm just worried about your guys lunch--"

"Oh please. I know how to make lunch Jane. I'm not that useless. What kind of dad would I be if I could not even prepare a meal for my kids." William said proudly.

I huffed once more, this time in annoyance. I knew that he was right, but I still couldn't help frowning as I looked down at the sight of Ellie and Noah. I looked at the clock and saw that I still have 20 minutes before the time that I promised to meet my office mates.

"Okay, I'll go but you have to promise me that you will call me if anything happens or if you just need me at home. I'll be on my way right away." I told William sternly.

William let out a laugh. "Oh thank god, she finally made up her mind!" he joked. I slapped his arm but he still had that amusing smile on his face. "Alright I'm sorry. Don't worry babe I'll call you if I need anything but you also have to promise me that you'll have fun with your friends and don't worry too much about us at home."

I nodded at his words even though I know that the moment I step out from the house I would probably call William to ask about the kids.

"I should get going now." I said as I get up from the couch, standing up on my toes and lean in to kiss my kids on their head. "Good bye kids, I'll be out for a while. Be good with your daddy, don't give your daddy a hard time okay. I love you two so much."

Both Noah and Ellie nodded their head with their eyes still fixed on the TV. They are probably addicted to the square size screen, I should bring them out more often I thought as I was shaking my head disapprovingly at my kids.

"I'll be leaving now. Promise you will call me if you need anything?" I asked William again as I looked at him in the eyes with my hands on his chest, savoring the feeling of his hard chest under my palm.

"Darling, stop worrying about us. Now go and have fun but not too much fun though. Don't want you to go home to another guy." William said playfully.

I chuckled. "I would rather go home to my husband."

William cupped my face in his hand and kiss me slowly. I closed my eyes for a moment and moaned.

"William..."

"Sorry, I will call to check up on you later. Have fun, we will be here when you get home." William said while letting me go.

I nodded my head while making my way to the front door. "I'll be back soo." I murmured.

William waved at me slightly. "Love you babe. Take care!"

"I love you Will." I smiled as I reluctantly grabbed my car keys. It took a few more minutes of me hesitating and William making a fuss before I finally got myself out the door and into my car. I am a little nervous about leaving William alone with the kids but also a bit excited for the time off.

-

I checked my phone again, probably for the fifteenth time, only to see no incoming call or message from William. I debated to call him but I don't want to miss the conversation that me and my friends currently having and I also don't want to hear a lecture from William on how paranoid I am being right now.

Don't blame me for over worrying. I know how tiring it is to watch over the kids and satisfy their needs so I really don't want William to go through it alone. I doubt he could handle them on his own. William might be a mighty CEO but he's still just a guy at heart and still learn how to cope in being a dad of two children.

I had to admit, caring for a baby was difficult. I still remember me and William had never felt exhaustion like it before after the birth of

Ellie. I had bags under my eyes like never before. Sometimes I would walk into the kitchen, baby in my arms, and catch my husband half asleep as he brewed the coffee for both of us.

It took it's toll on the both of us, but it was completely worth it. But that can't win over the times when I gave birth to Noah. I had nobody with me at the time. I was grateful enough to at least have Danny and his girlfriend-at-the-moment to look after me.

I always gave my one hundred percent into motherhood, and I was getting the hang of taking care of my two kids for sure. But there were times when William would have to kindly remind me to eat something before going to sleep because I hadn't eaten anything all day.

I laughed at the stories that one of my friend told us about our boss at the work place. I felt the least exhausted than I had in a long long time. All along, William had been right. It was exactly what I needed after working so hard.

A couple of hours later and I was ready to go back home to my family.

Once arrived, I fumbled a bit with the keys when I tried to open the front door. A few tries later I got the door open, and I shut it behind me quietly while putting down my keys. The house was silent. I didn't want to call out in case the kids were sleeping, so I slipped off my shoes and walked through the house carefully, trying to find my loved ones.

Once I found them, which is in the living room, the sight of them was precious enough to make me melt.

William and our daughter were both happy asleep on the couch. His chest was bare and he was wearing nothing but a pair of grey sweatpants. He looked exhausted and his lips were slightly parted, causing him to snore lightly. Meanwhile, Noah was sleeping soundly on the carpeted floor while hugging a pillow.

My baby girl was sleeping across William's bare chest, her little body fitting cozily into his embrace. His large hands were settled on her back as if to secure her there and I could see the rise and fall of her shoulders with every breath that she took. Her chubby little cheeks were pressing against William's skin and it almost made me giggle.

I tiptoed across the room and reached down to scoop my daughter up, settling her into my arms. She hardly stirred but as soon as I picked her up, William's eyes flashed open.

"Hm what?" he mumbled, still half asleep as he propped himself up on his elbows.

"Hey, it's okay we're good." I whispered, flashing him a small smile. I pressed a soft kiss to the top of Ellie's head, inhaling her scent gently.

"Babe can you pick Noah up?" I asked, looking at my little boy still sleeping.

"Yeah sure, you go ahead while I pick him up." William said.

I watched as William exhaled a soft yawn, reaching his arms up high into the air in a stretch before looking down at Noah. Even through the exhaustion, I could see the adoration that William had for Noah in the way he looked at him, and it brought a warmth to my chest that William still love Noah as much even after we had Ellie. I was lucky enough to have him in my life.

He scoop Noah in his arms and stood up from the carpeted floor, walking through the house towards the bedrooms with me. I entered Ellie's bedroom and slowly put her down on the bed. Meanwhile William walked into Noah's bedroom while I put my baby girl to sleep. I pratically holding my breath and praying that Ellie wouldn't stir or wake up. When she didn't I exhaled a breath of relief, reaching over to turn off the lights and walking out of her bedroom.

When I walked into my bedroom, I saw that William was sitting up in bed, scrolling through his phone with sleepy eyes.

"Hey handsome. Not sleep yet?" I asked, slipping on my pajama.

"I'm waiting for you." he said with a drowsy smile, placing his phone on his bedside table.

I simply smiled, walking over to sit on my side of the bed as I reached in an attempt to unhook my bra from underneath my t-shirt.

"Here babe, let me." William said, reaching for me. I scooched closer, brushing my hair aside to drape over one shoulder as his hands slid beneath my t-shirt. His fingers tickled my back as he unhooked my bra effortlessly. Once I felt it unhooked I pulled the straps out from my arms and pulled the garment out from under my shirt, turning to look at William with a cheeky grin.

"Well done, William."

"You can say I've had a lot practice." he grinned smugly, reaching to scoop me up against his chest with his broad arms. I giggled softly, snuggling into his side as I tangled my legs with his and nestled my head on his shoulder, craning my neck momentarily to press a soft kiss against his jaw.

"How was you day out?" William asked softly. My arm was draped over his bare chest, and he was running his fingertips up and down it.

"It was good and I had fun. You were right babe. I really needed it. Thank you Will." I admitted.

"See? I'm always right." he grunted softly, turning his head to bump his nose against mine.

"Nuh uh, don't push your luck babe." I snickered. "So how were the kids today?" My turn to ask.

"It was okay. The kids love me, I love them. We're living a happy family." William shrugged like it was nothing.

"Baby, I'm serious." I laughed at him.

William just chuckled as he pulled me closer against him, pressing a lingering kiss against the top of my head. "Everything was good darling. I told you I could handle them."

"Good for you then." I said sleepily as I closed my eyes and sighed contently. I felt myself becoming sleepier by the minute.

I'm almost asleep when William suddenly told me, "You know what babe, I asked Noah today to help me to look after her little sister. And then Ellie asked me when can she have her little sister too."

"But Will, I thought we agreed to wait a little longer after Ellie." I murmured sleepily, eyes still closed.

"Yeah I know. But I also remember you agree on having a soccer team with me." Even with eyes close I can already know he was smirking at me.

"Fine but not now. I want to sleep William." I said, rather groggily.

"Sure okay. But oh my god, babe can you imagine having a lot of kids enough to make our own soccer team? Letting them all wearing the same coloured jersey with a Winston written in the back. I can show them off at the office and let them play, running around the office hallway just to pissed of my staffs." William chuckled at his thoughts.

"I love you. I do. You got a nice imagination baby. But let's save it for later. Now sleep." I said with a triumph smile on my face. My husband is really something else.

"Oh honey that's not an imagination. That's a future I'm looking at, baby." William said before closing his eyes and join me to a content sleep.

Ingram Content Group UK Ltd.
Milton Keynes UK
UKHW022011030523
421159UK00014B/343